I0583607

Praise for
KRISTINE KATHRYN RUSCH'S
DIVING UNIVERSE

"The Diving Universe, conceived by Hugo-Award winning author Kristine [Kathryn] Rusch is a refreshingly new and fleshed out realm of sci-fi action and adventure."
—*Astroguyz*

"Kristine Kathryn Rusch is best known for her Retrieval Artist series, so maybe you've missed her Diving Universe series. If so, it's high time to remedy that oversight."
—*Analog*

"...a story of exploration of an artifact on an alien world, a bit reminiscent of the sort of story that Jack McDevitt writes."
—*Eyrie*

"...Denon is literally luminescent in its depiction."
—*Suite101*

"*The Spires* makes for a very good read."
—*SFRevu*

The Diving Universe
(Reading Order)

THE SPIRES OF DENON

A DIVING UNIVERSE NOVELLA

KRISTINE KATHRYN RUSCH

*wmg*PUBLISHING

The Spires of Denon

Copyright © 2019 Kristine Kathryn Rusch

All rights reserved

Published 2019 by WMG Publishing
www.wmgpublishing.com
First published in *Asimov's SF Magazine,* April/May 2009
Cover art copyright © Yvonne Less/Dreamstime
Book and cover design copyright © 2019 by WMG Publishing
Cover design by Allyson Longueira/WMG Publishing
ISBN-13: 978-1-56146-299-5
ISBN-10: 1-56146-299-3

*This book is licensed for your personal enjoyment only.
All rights reserved. This is a work of fiction. All characters and events
portrayed in this book are fictional, and any resemblance to real people
or incidents is purely coincidental. This book, or parts thereof, may not be
reproduced in any form without permission.*

THE SPIRES
OF DENON

A DIVING UNIVERSE NOVELLA

1

MEKLOS VERR TOOK OVER ONCE THE COMMAND SHIP entered Amnthra's atmosphere. He was a better on-planet pilot than anyone else on board. Besides, he preferred to do most things himself.

Even though he had the coordinates, Meklos flew hands-on. He opened the portals so that the cockpit, which jutted out in front of the small ship, seemed like it was encased in sky. He didn't have quite a three-hundred-and-sixty degree view, although it was close.

Only the area directly behind him, where a door led to the area the crew usually called the bunkhouse, blocked the view.

It had taken two days to get to Amnthra from base, and that was about twelve hours longer than any group should have been in this vessel. But no other space-to-ground vessel had been available on short notice, so he had to take this one.

This part of Amnthra was isolated and sparsely populated. According to rumor, the ancients still lived in these mountains. However, no matter how hard he looked, he couldn't find any independent confirmation of those rumors.

The Naramzin Mountain Range had some of the tallest peaks in this sector. It ran from east to west along Amnthra's largest continent. In fact, except for the beaches along the edge of the continent, the range and its small hidden valleys *were* Amnthra's largest continent.

Most of Amnthra's people now lived on islands and the four smaller continents, which were mostly flat. The weather was good in those places, the soil rich, and life spectacular.

Or so the travelogues told him.

They also told him to avoid the Naramzins. Hostile terrain of surprising beauty, the travelogues said. Easy to get lost in.

Easy to die in.

Meklos had no intention of dying.

He also had no intention of getting lost.

He was heading to the largest valley on the continent—the Valley of Conquerors—where he and his team would camp before they hiked to the Spires of Denon—and the city beneath them.

The Spires of Denon were the reason he had to leave the ship so far away. They were delicate, so delicate that scientists believed that the wrong harmonic vibration would shatter them, and one of the great treasures of the Lost Age would disappear forever.

He could see the Spires in the distance, rising like Earthmade skyscrapers into the clear blue sky.

Right now, he didn't care about the Spires. Right now, he worried about landing, hiking, and working under such restrictive conditions.

He had agreed to those conditions—had, in truth, hired on for them. But he didn't like them.

And he liked them less as the peaks of the Naramzin Range came into view. The Naramzin was unconquerable—that was what the ancient texts said, which was why the Denonites had, for a time, conquered every known civilization on Amnthra.

It wasn't until Amnthra got rediscovered by the other peoples in the sector that the Denonites actually got defeated.

And then they disappeared.

One of the great mysteries of the Lost Age.

And one he wasn't about to solve.

He was just here to provide security—not that he could find any real reason for it. He had done some research, in the limited time he had before taking this job, and it looked like no one and nothing threatened the group of archeologists who worked the ancient city of Denon.

His people needed a rest. They'd gone on a rescue mission two months before and found themselves in the middle of a civil war. Two weeks and four deaths later, they managed to rescue some university professors who had wandered into the wrong encampment.

He'd given the bulk of his team a vacation. Fifteen remained—the fifteen who, like him, didn't believe in time off.

So he'd force them to take it with this easy job in one of the great sites of the Lost Age.

He had a hunch he might even enjoy this job himself.

2

GABRIELLE REESE STOOD HIP-DEEP IN THE CHALK-covered water. The water was cold against her waders. Her hands were growing numb, which was the worst thing for this work. Even the tip of her nose was cold.

She stood on an unstable pile of rocks, which partially blocked the center arch in the underground caverns. She had wedged herself against the wall and what might have been a stone protecting a small cubby.

She could see the statue in the glare of her headlamp. The statue was small, black, and definitely not Denonite. If she had to guess, she would wager that the statue had come from one of the lost tribes, the ones that the Denonites had conquered early in their reign on Amnthra.

"Gabrielle," said Yusef Kimber, one of the best archeologists on her crew, "you have to get out of there. You're fifteen minutes past time."

Fifteen minutes past time. A time she had established, based on her own research. She hadn't allowed the medical doctor down here to do his own estimates.

So far, only she and Yusef even knew the caverns existed.

She didn't trust the rest of her team. If she told anyone else, they'd tell the graduate students, the post-docs, and the hangers-on who were digging out the ancient city.

Once those people knew, this place would be overrun with thieves, thrill seekers, and treasure hunters, not to mention journalists and art historians, who would want to see all this evidence of wars in the Lost Age.

"Gabrielle," Yusef said.

"All right," she said, letting the exasperation into her voice.

She reached into the niche and carefully grabbed the statue. It felt like it was made of ice, even though she knew it wasn't.

Her breath caught.

It was lovely—and she was right. It wasn't Denonite. It came from a completely different culture, one she hadn't seen outside of historical texts.

She waved her other hand at Yusef so that he could come down and take the statue. They hadn't found as much in the niches as she expected. Not all the niches were full. But enough of them were that she was convinced an entire treasure trove had once existed here.

The water posed the greatest problem. She knew they weren't very deep in the caverns. The flooding had probably taken artifacts and moved them out of their protective holes.

She could only hope that it hadn't ruined them as well.

Yusef wrapped the statue in protective covering and put it into his pack. They'd been storing everything in a hidden part of the building that covered the entrance to the caverns.

Soon she would have to move the items. She was preparing a nearby temple so that she could clean and identify them. Mostly, she planned to work alone.

But if she did bring in some of the other members of her team, she would tell them the items had come from the ground or the buildings inside the city, not from the caverns.

She placed her hands on the flat rock just above the waterline and pulled herself up, the way that she used to pull herself out of the full-grav pool on her father's starbase. She scraped her right wader against the stone, leaving a dank chalky mark.

She wasn't sure if that mark would be permanent or not. Damage was easy in these caverns—hell, it was easy everywhere in the ancient city, which had been untouched until her team had uncovered it five years before.

It had taken a lot of work, but she'd managed to keep the city quiet for two years. Finally, she needed more help, so she advertised on college boards all over the sector. She got dozens of graduate students, and a handful of post-docs. The post-docs were still here, but the graduate students cycled in and out like the itinerant students they were, bringing the news of the ancient city of Denon into the mainstream community.

Fortunately, she had published her early research before the ad. She would have to do the same thing with the caverns. But not until she explored them all and learned what other treasures were here.

She pulled her other knee up, making a second mark, then placed her hand on the side of the arch. This time, she didn't leave a mark. But the stone was cold, even through her glove. She was going to have to sit in the sun for a long time to get this chill out of her system.

Still, she wasn't quite ready to leave. Before she walked to the old path that led to the steps, she peered through the arch.

She had hoped to get inside that next cavern before her time elapsed, and she hadn't made it. But she had learned something. The floor slanted upwards, so the next series of caverns—if, indeed, there were a series—would not yet be underwater.

The light from her miner's helmet shone inside, reflecting off the natural white walls. She didn't see inky blackness below, which was how the water manifested itself in the darkness—even when the water had taken on the sludge from the walls.

A pristine cavern—maybe the last pristine cavern—before the underwater work began.

3

THE AIR WAS DRIER HERE THAN MEKLOS EXPECTED, AND the sunlight brighter. He'd never seen sunlight this bright. When he'd asked Chavo Grennoble, the young man the archeologists had sent to lead the team up the correct path, Chavo had said that the brightness was a change in perception, which came because Meklos had so recently been on a ship.

Meklos had been on many ships before landing planetside, and he'd never experienced light like this before. But he said nothing, even though his own second in command Phineas Aussiere gave him an odd look.

Meklos had been on jobs filled with academics before. They always condescended to him, assuming he was stupid because he preferred a physical job to sitting in some classroom letting someone else tell him what to think.

He adjusted his pack along his shoulders. In it, he had an automatic tent, rations for the next month, and more equipment than he probably needed. He hadn't been able to assess the job from the starbase, so he had brought collapsible bots, motion detectors, sound detectors and a variety of cameras. He also had sixteen self-assembling laser rifles, several Grow-it grenades, and one giant sky cannon.

Even though everything was in its inert or collapsed state, he was still carrying thirty-five kilos on his back. He carried the greatest weight because he had the sky cannon, but his team's packs weren't much lighter.

The kid, Chavo, was scrambling up the path like a mountain goat, and the entire team was keeping up with him. Meklos knew for a fact that the kid wouldn't have been able to walk this path with thirty-five kilos on his back.

Meklos thought of asking the kid how they'd gotten their equipment over this peak, then realized that the kid wouldn't know. From what little Meklos had learned before agreeing to the job, the project started ten years before with an examination of the Spires of Denon, and then turned into an excavation of the entire ancient city nestled in the center of the mountain itself.

As they got closer to the peak, the air grew warmer. Meklos had thought it would be colder. On inhabited worlds, most mountains, particularly those this tall, had a snowpack at the top.

In fact, he had thought this mountain—called Denon's Secret—had a snowpack. From the valley where they'd left the ship, he had noted the reddish-brown dirt slowly turning white near the Spires. He had naturally assumed snow.

But no snow could survive in this heat. If he had known it was going to be this warm, he would have worn some environmental gear.

The ground beside him was turning white, which was how he knew they were nearing the top. From this angle, it was nearly impossible to look at the Spires. They loomed above him, large and imposing.

Their shadows crisscrossed the path, like the shadows of branches in a forest. But unlike the shadows of branches, these shadows were huge. He would step out of a shadow into the sunlight, and walk for several meters before stepping into another shadow.

The Spires weaved and bent into each other, adding at least four more kilometers to the top of the mountain. As he neared the peak, he couldn't tell if this mountain was old and rounded with time or if—in some distant past— the mountaintop had blown off.

If it had blown off, then he was climbing a volcano which unnerved him slightly. He'd worked two separate jobs near active volcanoes and their rumblings kept him awake at night.

But nothing in his research claimed Denon's Secret was an active volcano. If it had been, the Spires would not have survived. The groundquakes would have shattered them.

The team had nearly reached the Spires when Chavo stopped. He extended his spindly arms as if he were some religious figure leading his followers to the promised land.

"Before we go farther," he said, "I need to tell you the rules of the Spires. I'm sure that Gabrielle or someone else below will reiterate, but since we're going to go right past them, I figured I'd better say something."

"Could've said it at the base," someone muttered behind Meklos.

"He thinks we're too dumb to remember for that long," someone else answered, echoing Meklos's thoughts.

Chavo didn't seem to hear or if he did, the comments didn't embarrass him—probably because he believed them to be true.

He glanced behind him, then swept his hand toward the upper part of the mountain.

"The Spires are manmade," Chavo said. "They're hand carved. They've been treated with something—we don't know what—that has allowed them to remain in place for hundreds, maybe thousands, of years. In addition to being bent and formed by hand, the Spires are also etched."

Meklos didn't know that. He raised his head a little, and saw the edges of the Spires coming out of the white dirt.

He couldn't imagine that sort of painstaking work. He wasn't even sure how the creators made it. Did they begin at the top and add pieces as they went along, until they had the full-sized Spires? Then did they take them from whatever workshop they'd used and attached them to the mountainside?

The technology needed to do this seemed beyond the ancients. But the ancients had built and forgotten more technology than he would ever know. After all, geneticists proved beyond any doubt that this sector was colonized by people from Earth, just like the stories said. The DNA matches were complete.

Which meant that everyone in the sector had common ancestors, at least once upon a time. That time was so long ago that civilizations rose and fell, knowledge was lost, knowledge was gained, and wars were fought, then forgotten.

Just like the history of colonization had been forgotten.

"So," Chavo said, "because they're unusually delicate, don't touch the Spires. We're afraid that the oils from your fingertips could harm the coating."

"Why?" someone muttered. "Because of where we've been?"

"They don't know where we've been," someone else said. "That's what they're afraid of."

"Actually," Chavo said loudly—since he'd clearly heard that, "none of us is allowed to touch. We've seen them forever and examined them for ten years, and we still can't touch. We can't figure out how to study them without dismantling one, and that would be a crime."

Not to mention that it might undermine the entire Spire system.

"So we take readings and try to examine with what equipment we have. Even that we have to be careful with. We don't dare use powerful equipment near the Spires. We're too afraid to damage them. What we're hoping for is that we'll find some pieces in the city below, and then we can do a proper study, but so far, we haven't found anything."

It almost sounded like a tourist guide spiel, except that Meklos knew tourists never came here.

He found it curious that they couldn't figure out anything about the Spires. The lack of knowledge, even after a decade of study, made him realize that all those precautions the academics had presented him with were just that: precautions. They were based on guesses, not actual knowledge.

He wondered what they all would think if they knew how many weapons he was bringing into their stronghold. He would wager that they would disapprove.

They were probably taking so long on this dig because they couldn't use some of the normal tricks of the trade— sonic cleaners set on a level for delicate work and large equipment to carry dirt and debris out of this area.

"Is this the only path?" Meklos asked.

"It's the only one we use," Chavo said.

"That wasn't my question," Meklos said. "We're here to protect you and your dig. We need to know if there are other ways to access it."

Chavo glanced over his shoulder again, as if someone were watching him. As he turned back, he bit his lower lip.

"There are lots of paths over the peak and through the Spires. This is the only one that is accessible."

"To whom?" Meklos asked. "To your people? Or to machinery? Or to anyone with climbing experience?"

Chavo shrugged. "Honestly, I don't know. This is the only one I've ever used."

"How long have you been here?" Meklos asked.

"Two years," Chavo said. "My post-doc focuses on the architecture of the city of Denon as it evolved—"

"Couldn't you study that from some library somewhere?" Phineas asked, obviously unable to contain his contempt any longer.

"I'm an archeologist, and an art historian," Chavo said with no little bit of pride. "This is an area of study that combines both of my disciplines."

"Well, you're testing our discipline," Meklos said. "We're wearing thirty-five kilograms on our backs and it's hot up here. We'd like to get to that city, find where we're going to camp, and eat a little something."

"No kidding," said one of the voices from the back.

Chavo looked at the pack on Meklos's back as if seeing it for the first time.

"Sorry," he said. "You might have to take that off as we cross the peak. The arch beneath this part of the Spires is pretty narrow."

Meklos frowned. Obviously, then, the original teams hadn't used this path to lug their equipment in.

Chavo climbed ahead of them, waiting near the arch, which barely reached the top of his head. When Meklos joined him, Chavo pointed up. "Your pack gonna hit that?"

"Of course not," Meklos said, but he paused anyway, not because he was uncertain, but because he wanted to get a good look at the Spires up close.

The arch wasn't a true arch. Instead, it was part of the weave. Several branches came together at this point. Two twisted above Meklos to form an even larger pattern. Two more branched in from the sides, giving the arch itself a four-point base.

The trail went below that base.

"I'm going to make sure the others won't hit it," Chavo said. "So go ahead."

"They'll be fine," Meklos said.

Chavo looked nervously at the rest of the team, climbing single-file behind Meklos, then back at Meklos.

Meklos raised his eyebrows. "After you," he said.

Chavo swallowed, then nodded. He clearly didn't want to go first, but he didn't see any choice.

Meklos smiled to himself. The kid was finally becoming intimidated.

Chavo walked under the arch, then eased himself down the side of the mountain. The trail had to have gotten steep there. Meklos made a mental note of that.

He followed, going slowly, not because he was afraid of hitting the arch, but because he wanted to look at it as he passed.

Chavo wasn't kidding—the Spires had etchings. So far as Meklos could see, each etching was different. Some appeared to be characters, like letters or numbers, and others were drawings. He noted one as he passed, a woman standing beneath this very arch, or something quite similar to it.

He only had to hunch slightly as he walked through the arch. He had plenty of clearance. Even if he hadn't, his pack would have flattened itself against his back to avoid touching anything. It was a design feature he neglected to tell Chavo.

The kid didn't need to know everything.

Once Meklos got through the arch, the path turned sharply to the right. That was why Chavo had braced himself as he came through. There were more parts to the arch, some actually flattened before Meklos, like a floor.

The path swerved to avoid all of that.

The floor had etchings as well, but he couldn't see them clearly from the path.

What surprised him was that they weren't covered with dust or dirt. Just one day on this mountaintop should have kept that floor covered in the whitish material that surrounded them.

He swerved with the path, then walked down four steps. Chavo was waiting for him on a stone platform, one that was not part of the Spires. Meklos stopped beside Chavo, then looked up the mountainside. His team was coming through, one at a time, each examining the Spires as they walked, each showing the same amount of curiosity he had.

"The city's just down there," Chavo said, with no small amount of pride.

Meklos looked. The city sprawled below them as if it had always been exposed to the sun, as if teams of archeologists hadn't uncovered it in the past five years.

Some of the dirt remained along the edges, more, it seemed to Meklos, to prevent climbers from going through the Spires the wrong way than as any integral part of the dig.

But the dirt did show how deeply the city had once been buried.

It filled the hollow in the mountain. White buildings, some small, and several quite large, scattered before him. They glimmered in the sunlight.

He realized then that some of the brightness had come from the reflected light off the white substance on the side of the mountain. Add to that the city itself, and his eyes actually hurt.

"Lovely, isn't it?" Chavo asked.

"Astonishing," Meklos said, and meant it. He had seen a lot of amazing things in his career, but never anything like this.

"Wait until you see it up close," Chavo said.

Meklos frowned. He had heard about the ancient city of Denon in school—everyone had. So many of this sector's myths and stories had come from here.

The city itself had survived several sieges.

As he looked at it now, though, the idea of surviving a siege here made him shudder. With a more powerful enemy on the mountainside, the inhabitants of the city would not stand a chance.

"Ready?" Chavo asked, leading Meklos to yet another set of stairs.

Meklos nodded. Places usually didn't make him uncomfortable, but this one did.

And he wasn't entirely sure why.

4

NAVI SALVINO CLASPED HER HANDS BEHIND HER BACK and studied the holographic map floating above the table. She had walked around it now a dozen times, zooming in, zooming out, and still she couldn't decide what to do.

The Naramzin Mountain Range looked formidable all by itself, but the strictures on landing anywhere near the Spires of Denon made this job almost impossible.

She wouldn't be able to get her people into the city of Denon without being seen. She certainly couldn't use weapons, and the newest strictures, made by the Monuments Protection Arm of the Unified Governments of Amnthra, restricted most forms of scanning equipment as well.

The Unified Governments had been suing Scholars Exploration for ownership of the mountaintop itself. Scholars Exploration had used a loophole in some of the local laws to claim ownership of the mountaintop.

Apparently the Unified Governments had never designed the Spires a protected area, which was a major mistake.

The Scholars took advantage of major mistakes. They'd become the bully in the sector, at least when it came to research sites.

In the beginning, the Scholars had simply been a way for sector universities to protect their research. A dozen universities had founded Scholars Exploration to give them some clout with the various sector governments. A variety of donors, many wealthy alumni, had provided start-up funding for the company decades ago. That start-up money had become a large fortune, thanks to the funds generated by patents, copyrights, sales of land and items made and/or found by the various scholars.

Most people saw the Scholars as a boon to knowledge throughout the sector. Navi saw them as a pain in the ass.

She walked around the table yet again. The mountaintop rose as if it had been carved there.

The Spires rose above the white mountaintop, hopelessly delicate. On one of her passes, she had counted sixteen spires, but it was hard to gauge, since they twisted and twined into each other. One branch would rise into a point, while another part of it forked away, wrapping itself around another spire.

The highest spire stood alone for several meters, white and shining in the simulation, as if lit from within.

If this holographic map was even half as impressive as the Spires themselves, then they were something to behold.

She pressed a button on her wristband, summoning this job's expert. She hated the experts. They were self-important little people who often felt slighted by being left out of some Scholars Exploration expedition.

This particular expert, Jonas Zeigler, hid his disappointment well, but Navi could still feel it, as if she had caused it.

The double doors slid open and he stepped inside, stopping as he gazed on the map. His black bangs flopped over the left side of his narrow face. He wore faded jeans and a cotton top, even though Navi kept her ship at regulation temperature—which meant it was cool, even for her.

He was a full professor of antiquities and art history at a tiny college at the edge of the sector. His speeches, his dissertation, and his annual works brought him to Navi's attention. Even though he didn't have a prestige position, he was considered the sector's foremost authority on the Spires—or he had been until Scholars had discovered the City of Denon in the hollow below them.

Zeigler had predicted that find in his now-famous dissertation, published nearly a decade before anyone thought to look for the city. But his tiny college couldn't afford to buy into Scholars, and so he wasn't qualified to lead an expedition into the area.

"You act like you've never seen the Spires." She had to walk behind him and wave her hand at the door, closing it. He hadn't moved since he stepped inside.

He shook himself, then took a deep breath. "Not like that," he said. "My school doesn't have the funds for such a sophisticated holounit."

"But you've seen them up close," she said. As a fifteen-year-old, he had hiked up Denon's Secret with his family, long before any archeologists had taken interest in the Spires.

"Up close you can hardly take in a single branch. The entire thing is impossible to see." He finally walked toward the map. "Although…."

"Although?" She hated the way he spoke, as if his thoughts raced ahead and he didn't feel as if he had to articulate all of them.

"Although they're much brighter in person. They are so white it actually hurts your eyes." He sounded wistful.

Sometimes places got a hold on people, made them almost worshipful. She'd seen it countless times—people willing to defend a small patch of ground that looked like nothing to her, because it meant something to them.

She hadn't suspected Zeigler of such an attitude, although someone else might have. It took her longer than most to recognize worshipful.

She had never worshipped anything. Her work was everything to her, had been since she left home at thirteen. She hadn't even fallen in love. Someone would mention a new job, and she would take it, for the challenge mostly, since money and perks didn't matter much to her.

"Last night," she said to Zeigler, "you mentioned something. You said you didn't think the security team would have been hired to protect the city. What did you mean?"

The words had echoed in her head since that moment. The security team had triggered her trip to Amnthra.

Even though the Scholars had hired the security team, the request for security hadn't originated with the Scholars.

The request had come directly from the surface itself.

Navi's computer systems were set up to automatically flag actions like that. She'd been monitoring nearly two hundred Scholars projects and sites all over the sector, and whenever something unusual happened, she got flagged.

This one intrigued her, because the city had been discovered so recently and it was hard to reach.

Historic places that were hard to reach and relatively new to the academic community were often rich with treasures.

Zeigler was still looking at the Spires.

His silence exasperated her. She asked, "Do you think the team was hired to protect the Spires?"

He gave her a look of such panic that she actually regretted the question.

"They're too beautiful to cut up," he said, which wasn't an answer to her question. The fact that he had thought of cutting them up meant someone else probably had as well.

"Could they be sold in parts?" she asked.

He let out a heavy sigh. It sounded almost mournful.

"Anything can be sold in parts," he said.

"So that's what you meant," she said. "You think the team was hired to protect the Spires."

He shook his head, but said no more.

"Then why do you think they hired the team?" she asked.

"The museum," he said after a moment.

His tone implied that she knew what the museum was.

She knew of countless museums. Some were attached to the universities. Some were in the wealthier cities throughout the sector. The Scholars had been making noise for years about starting a universal museum, one in the center of the sector, like a space port, complete with restaurants, hotels, and condos. The entire thing could be expanded as the Scholars found more items to put into it.

"Which museum?" she asked when he became clear he wasn't going to elaborate.

He whirled toward her, his face more animated than she had ever seen it.

"I thought you studied my work," he snapped. "You said you were familiar with it."

"I am," she said. She hadn't studied his work; that would have taken too much time. But she had scanned the précis and listened to his detractors as well as his supporters. She learned all she could about him as quickly as she could.

She simply hadn't had time to familiarize herself with the work itself.

"Everything I've done in the past six years has been about the museum," he said.

"The last six years, you talked about the history of Denonites," she said. "I recall nothing about a museum."

His face flushed. "You listened to the critics. You didn't listen to me."

She sighed, then extended her hands flat, in a gesture of peace. "Guilty," she said. "I don't have the patience for scholarship."

He glared at her, then turned his back on her. He continued to study the Spires.

"So what did the critics miss?" she asked.

"A discovery equal to that of the city itself," he said.

He answered her quicker than she had expected him to. She had thought he would nurse his anger a bit longer, but he hadn't.

"Why would they ignore that?"

"Because I'm not on-site," he said. "But I wasn't on-site when I figured out the city's location either."

"So tell me about the museum," she said.

He turned, his expression open. She didn't like the mood swing. She kept her back straight, her face impassive. She wasn't going to encourage this kind of emotionalism—although she would remember it.

He said, "The ancient texts all talked about the spoils of war. The Denonites went to war not for the conquest, but for the spoils."

So did many communities, she almost said, but remembered: It was better not to have a dialogue with Zeigler. It would derail him.

"Most scholars," he was saying, "believe the spoils are the standard ones—slaves, property, maybe extending the gene pool. But it always seemed to me to be more than that."

She frowned.

Zeigler reached toward the Spires. He touched them. The hologram encased his fingers.

"I always thought that any people who could create something that beautiful would appreciate beauty. The city

25

bears this out. The new documentation shows that it uses classical designs—ancient Earth designs—in its most prominent buildings."

Then he closed his hand into a fist and pulled it away from the Spires.

Navi nodded, to encourage him to continue.

"The Denonites lived in a small community," he said. "It's a jewel. They sent their own undesirables away, let them run the conquered cities. Nothing in the texts talk about slaves or massive troops moving back toward Denon's Secret. There is no mention of a place to keep prisoners or a place to ritually humiliate the losers of any war. So I spent the last few years asking myself this: If they didn't want the traditional spoils, what did they want?"

She was going to be here all day while he explained how he came to his conclusions. God, she hated academics.

"Then I discovered a mention of the caverns," he said.

Suddenly he had her attention.

"Caverns honeycomb that mountain. I think that's how the Denonites survived their many sieges. They weren't in the city when it got attacked. They were below it or beside it or maybe not even in it, if the caverns led to places outside of the mountain."

Her breath caught. Marvelous. The caverns would give her a way into the city, a way that could avoid the Spires entirely.

"Do you have proof of this?" she asked.

"Not exact proof," he said.

And she felt her heart sink.

"But," he added, "the texts mention the networks a lot, and then they mention the honeycombs. Only one of those references is in connection with a cavern, but that's enough. Because if you look at the Spires, what could they be, but a giant map?"

She frowned, and looked at the Spires. They seemed like artwork to her—a way of marking the city long before anyone arrived at it.

A monument, something that a culture built because it could.

"A map?" she asked, letting the disbelief into her voice.

"Surround it, not with air, but with dirt," he said. "Then what does it look like?"

She had to squint to imagine that. Then she shook her head.

"It's a network of caves," he said, "with exit points."

She wanted him to be right. She *needed* him to be right. But she didn't believe he was right. Everything he told her was too disjointed.

"But how does that tie to a museum?" she asked.

"It *is* the museum," he said.

He shoved his hand back into the middle of the hologram.

"This part," he said. "This maze-like network in the center, would be the best place to store artifacts stolen from other cultures. And if the caves look like the Spires, then they're white. Anything with color would jump off the walls, and stand out, even in a large space. Imagine it. It would be the best museum in the sector. Better even than that thing the Scholars are proposing because everything in this place would be ancient, and from cultures long gone."

That was the problem. She could imagine it. The wealth would be beyond measure.

Immediately her mind turned to the task at hand. "They would need more than fifteen people and some tech to guard this place."

"If they know what they have which I don't think they do," he said. "They stumbled onto the city. They weren't looking at my work. It was an accident."

"You think they have no idea how far these things extend.

He nodded. "And, since scans from above are limited by law, they have no way to find out."

She turned to the Spires, squinting, trying to see what he saw.

A map.

Navi smiled.

If Zeigler was right, he had just given her a way in.

5

THEY ACTIVATED THEIR TENTS ON A FLAT PART OF THE mountainside half a kilometer above the city.

From this vantage, they could see the city itself—all parts of it—and they would remember that they were here to guard it. Meklos still hadn't figured out how he was going to deploy his people and his equipment. He needed better maps for that. He also needed to know what exactly he'd been hired to protect.

If it was a single building, then he'd send his people there in shifts as well as keep a few stationed near the Spires. If it was the entire city itself, he might need reinforcements.

This area was vast, something that he hadn't realized when he took the job. It wasn't vast in area, so much as in sprawl. And it would be difficult to guard against a motivated invader, someone who wanted inside, someone to whom the rules about the Spires of Denon meant nothing.

He had one other problem as well. No one had warned him about how bright it was here. Even with proper equipment, the whiteness of the Spires, combined with the white shale on the mountainside and the white buildings below, created a kind of bleary-eyed exhaustion that he hadn't experienced outside of snow countries.

If he kept his people on shift too long or if they were stationed in the wrong spot, they might experience a kind of snow blindness.

And he hadn't checked the planet's cycle in relation to its sun. He had no idea if they would move closer while he was stationed here.

If so, the sun would grow brighter, and so would the light.

Even if he sent for better equipment, he still would have to station his people at their posts for half a normal shift. Which meant he would be understaffed.

He wished he'd been able to inspect the site before he arrived, just like he had asked to do. But Scholars Exploration, which had hired him, had said the site was too remote to justify the expense.

Then they had tripled his fee.

He'd noted the contradiction, and he understood the reason for it. They didn't want anyone who wasn't on their payroll near the site.

And that had piqued his curiosity.

This whole job had—partly because of the Spires themselves.

6

GABRIELLE STEPPED BACKWARDS, TOWARD THE OPEN doorway, and stuck her hands in her back pockets. The temple's main floor extended away from her, fading away into darkness.

Except for the front entrance, which had no door—and hadn't been designed for one, the temple had sealable doors and no windows.

Perfect for storage.

It was the largest building in the ancient city, a giant rectangle that stood in the exact center. All the main roads (the ones that the archeologists could clearly define as roads) led to this one spot.

She called it a temple, but there was no evidence that the Denonites were particularly religious. It was just that in previous ancient societies, buildings with this general shape and focus always ended up being the center of the religion.

Yusef believed it was some kind of government building, but he couldn't suggest what kind.

The main floor was one long open space. There wasn't even an altar or a place with a rise so that someone could stand above a crowd and make speeches.

The walls were plain white, like the exterior walls, but the floor was a marvel all by itself.

It was an inlaid replica of the Spires of Denon. As the careful cleaning commenced, she realized that the floor's design wasn't white against blue like she had initially thought. The Spires went from a warm reddish color to lighter shades of rose finally becoming a faint white. Only near the top, where the Spires supposedly touched the sun, did the drawing itself become a spectacular white.

She had initially planned on covering the floor, but she wasn't sure whether or not it would ruin the artwork. Her specialists thought that even a raised floor could scratch the image below.

So she had to be careful. On the areas where there was no artwork, she had installed a raised floor. She would put up half walls around those areas. She needed them for the final cleaning, sorting and classification. Then the artifact, whatever it was, would get moved to the correct part of the floor until it could go to its assigned destination.

The problem, of course, would be the larger items. She wasn't even sure where to store them, let alone how to work with them.

And if she had to remove any of them from the city...

She shook her head. She had already commandeered a couple of buildings near the temple, but none were as sturdy.

One of the post-docs suggested leaving the larger artifacts where she found them, which sounded well and good, until they tried to deal with the artifacts in the flooded part of the caverns.

Not that she knew for certain there were artifacts in that part of the cavern. Even though the guards had shown up, the special cave divers she sent for were delayed on some other job.

Someone touched her arm, and she jumped.

She turned. Yusef stood next to her, his eyes twinkling.

She had been so deep in thought, she hadn't even heard him approach.

"What?" she asked.

"The guards you hired," he said, "they want to talk to you."

She suppressed a sigh. The last thing she wanted to do was talk to a group of guards.

She hadn't given them much thought. She had asked the Scholars to hire some security guards and to make sure they weren't thugs. She didn't want careless people blundering their way through the delicate parts of the city.

If she had been able to afford it, she would have hired them herself. But she'd had her hands full with hiring the cave divers. She didn't want the Scholars to know she had even found caves, until she knew exactly what those caves were and what treasures they contained.

She sighed. She didn't want to deal with the guards, but she was clearly going to have to.

"Where are they?" she asked.

"He," said a voice behind her. "And he's right here."

She turned.

The man who stood behind her wasn't as large as she would have expected a guard to be. He was not much taller than she was, and his muscles looked real, not the enhanced kind that made him seem like he had inserted cotton under his skin. His hair was a little too long, and his dark eyes were wary.

"I'm Meklos Verr," he said. "I'm in charge of the security team."

She didn't have to ask where the rest of the team was. That was obvious. She had seen the automated tents blossom on the inside of the crater. They weren't too far from her initial base camp.

"Gabrielle Reese," she said. "I'm the person in charge of this mess."

He glanced at the entrance behind him. "It's much less of a mess than I expected."

"We've had years on the upper layer of the city, but there's so much more work to be done."

He nodded, then looked at Yusef. The look held dismissal, and just a little contempt.

She put her hand on Yusef's arm. If she hadn't, he would have left without Meklos saying a word.

That was power. Amazing that such a slight man in such an unimportant position had it.

"I need to talk with you about the security arrangements," Meklos said.

She nodded, but didn't let go of Yusef's arm.

"I think the fewer who are privy to them the better." Meklos's tone made it sound like what he had just said was the opening salvo in a conversation, not a cue to dismiss Yusef.

She had to give it a second of consideration. Normally, she would include Yusef in any conversation. But Yusef seemed to make the guard uncomfortable. It was just easier to do what the guard wanted. Then they could be done with this conversation.

She let go of Yusef's arm. "It's all right. I'll join everyone for lunch in about an hour."

Yusef flushed. He gave Meklos a furtive glance, frowned, and then scurried off.

Gabrielle had never seen Yusef move like that. It took her a few moments to realize that Meklos actually scared him.

"You scared him," she said in wonder.

Meklos's eyes moved slightly. She had a feeling she had surprised him.

"Very good," he said. "Most people wouldn't have noticed."

"It was pretty obvious," she said. "I've never seen him react like that."

"Hm," Meklos said. It wasn't an answer. It wasn't even really a word. It was, however, a dismissal, as if her opinion didn't count for much.

"Are you going to do that all the time?" she asked.

"Scare your people?" he asked.

She nodded.

He shrugged. "Depends on if it's part of my job."

"Your job is to guard the dig," she said.

"That's what it said on the hire." He shifted his weight slightly, without moving his feet. "But I'm not sure what that means. Or who I'm guarding it from."

She frowned. She hadn't expected to have to talk to him. She had expected him and his team to get to work the moment they arrived.

Clearly the Scholars hadn't explained this job to them. Of course, how hard could a guard job be?

She mentally shrugged. People with Meklos's job were, by definition, not that bright. So she would explain it.

"All right," she said. "Here's what we need. You need to protect us from anyone who wants to see the city. At the moment, anyone can view the Spires—from a safe distance. We—"

"Which is?" he asked.

He had derailed her train of thought. "Excuse me?"

"What's the safe distance?"

She frowned at him. "You were told the distances when you arrived. The protected area begins at the base of the mountain. No one can climb it and no one can come near the Spires. They're fragile."

"They don't look fragile," he said. "Up close they look amazingly sturdy."

"They're fragile," she repeated. He was irritating her. She didn't like her statements questioned.

He opened his hands in a conciliatory gesture. "All right," he said. "They're fragile."

She crossed her arms.

"Go on," he said.

She had lost her place. He had asked what the rules for protection were. She sighed deeply, then nodded once.

"No one comes up the mountainside without our permission. No one gets into the city without our permission."

"Okay," he said. "Got that. What else?"

"Soon we'll be taking some items from the city to another site for cleaning, grading and inspection. We're going to need protection for those operations."

"Another site," he said. "On Amnthra?"

Her cheeks had grown warm. "Where that site is doesn't matter right now."

"Oh, but it does," he said. "Because if we're making a land trip, we'll need the right equipment. It'll probably take longer. If we're using some kind of jumper to get across the planet, then we'll need to know weight limits. We may need an extra jumper or two so that we have the correct amount of personnel and equipment going with the items. Honestly, the more I know, the better job I'll do."

She didn't want him to know. She didn't want him in the middle of her work.

She would wait to tell him details like until the time came. Maybe by then, she would know how to control him.

"We'll make the plans for item removal later," she said. "It's not something we need to think about now."

"Well," he said. "We might want to, because if we require help or additional equipment—"

"I said, we don't need to think about it now."

He stared at her for a moment. His entire expression had gone flat. "All right."

"We're done now," she snapped.

He shook his head just once. "I'm sorry, Ms. Reese—Dr. Reese? Gabrielle?"

"Dr. Reese," she said, even though everyone on her team called her Gabrielle.

"Dr. Reese," he said. "I still have a lot of questions."

"I don't have time for them," she said.

"Then who do I talk to? Because we're not starting work until these questions are answered."

She bit her lower lip so hard she could taste blood, something she hadn't done in a long time. "I think you've forgotten, Meklos, that you work for me."

"Actually, no, I don't, Dr. Reese." His voice was calm. That galled her. While she was furious at him, he didn't seem to have any emotions concerning her at all. "If you check the agreement—"

"I didn't see the agreement. That's between you and Scholars."

"It's about you and how our operations run," he said. "Once security understands its job, we take precedence. If we tell you the area needs to be evacuated immediately, you evacuate immediately. If we tell you that we have proof someone is a threat, that someone—no matter how valuable they appear—will leave the premises. If you would like a copy of the agreement, I can have it sent directly to you. I'm not sure exactly where you'd like it—"

"I'll get a copy from the Scholars." Her cheeks were hot now, and had to be bright red. There was no way to hide how angry he had made her.

"Good," he said. "You'll see that I'm right. So, in the spirit of cooperation, let me ask a few more questions."

She sighed heavily so that he understood what an inconvenience this all was.

"I need to know how much access we get to the site." He waited as if he expected an answer to that immediately.

"What do you mean, access?"

"Are we allowed in the dig sites? Can we get off the paths near the Spires without damaging something important?"

She waved a hand. She had no idea, and she wasn't about to tell him that. So she said, "Just list your questions. I'll answer the ones I can right now, and I'll send you to the right people for the others."

"All right." His back straightened, as if she had finally upset him. "I need to know whether we protect from the air as well as the ground. I need to know if we pay attention to ships in orbit. I need to know if we monitor communications—"

"My god," she said. "It'll take half my life to direct you people. I just wanted some guards."

He ignored that and continued as if she hadn't spoken. "I need to know who you think wants to get onto this site, and if those people have theft or sabotage in mind. I need to know if anyone's life has been threatened."

"Sabotage?" she asked, feeling cold. "You think someone might come in here and ruin this?"

"I don't think anything, Dr. Reese. I need to know what your concerns are. Most importantly, I need to know which members of your staff and crew we can trust, which ones we need to monitor, and which ones we need to watch zealously."

She felt a little woozy. She must have been holding her breath.

"This is not what I expected when I told Scholars to hire you," she said.

"What did you expect?" he asked.

"That you'd come in, stand guard, and let us get on with our work."

"We'll do that, ma'am," he said. "Just as soon as we know what we're guarding, who we're guarding it from, and how much access we have."

She hadn't given it any thought at all. Did she want his people to guard the city itself or just the access routes? And what were the access routes?

And then there was the question of her staff and crew. She didn't trust any of them. She never told them anything except what they needed to know.

At the same time, she trusted them implicitly. She sent them to work on sites without supervision. She wasn't sure how to explain the contradiction to this man.

"I take it your behavior is not unusual for your line of work," she said to him.

That thin smile rose on his lips. This time, he didn't try to hide the contempt.

"If you want to hire someone else, go ahead," he said. "Just remember, in your initial communiqué with Scholars, you asked for the best security team they could find."

She didn't ask for that. All she had asked for were some guards. Obviously, someone in Scholars figured she needed more than simple guards.

Dammit.

He was saying, "They found us. Whoever they send next may not ask as many questions, may not be as annoying from the start, but they may not be as good either."

She wasn't sure she cared about good. She wasn't sure she cared about any of this at all.

But he was here. They were here. They'd do as she asked when the time came. Until then, she would stall.

"I don't think of my people the way you want me to," she said.

He said, "Then maybe it's time you start."

7

NAVI FINALLY FORCED HERSELF TO LOOK AT ZEIGLER'S scholarly works. Since she and her team were orbiting Amnthra waiting for something to come out of the City of Denon—more communications, maybe items in transit, maybe the arrival of more security—she didn't have a lot to do except think.

And she'd been thinking a great deal since her conversation with Zeigler.

She kept staring at the holomap. She had brightened the Spires so that they looked almost blinding, although Zeigler said even that wasn't correct. Then she had two of her assistants look through geologic records to see if anyone had mapped caves in the Naramzin Mountain Range.

The mountains, it turned out, were mostly unexplored—or at least, they hadn't been explored in the modern era. Only mountain climbers, adventurers, and extreme athletes had gone up there until the archeologists and scholars descended upon the Spires of Denon as if they were some kind of holy relic.

She couldn't even tell what caused the descent—whether it was some scholarly discovery or a meeting or something that happened in passing.

Zeigler's research was meticulous. She had started with the works he'd published six years ago, and worked her way forward. She didn't care as much about his hypothesis about the City of Denon, the hypothesis that had turned out to be right, although she probably should have. Because if he used similar logic and proof to find the caverns, then she could really trust his conclusions.

Only she somewhat trusted them now, and she barely had the patience to go through the six years of research. The idea of going over his entire life's work gave her the shudders.

Zeigler made his presentations in lectures, holovids, actual documents, and at conferences where his words were recorded, as well as the question and answer sessions. All of his raw research was easily accessible, unlike some she'd seen. Some scholars made it hard to dig through the raw materials, but Zeigler clearly wasn't afraid of someone stealing his positions.

He obviously wanted his work to be transparent, so that the other scholars would realize how correct he was.

It took her days to go through the material, and she still wasn't done. But she was convinced: there were caverns beneath the City of Denon.

The problem was, she had her ship's sensors go over the mountain range. The area around the Spires was blocked. Every time a sensor touched the area, the stream got bounced back to her ship with a warning:

Energy of any kind could destroy a valuable part of Amnthra. The Spires of Denon are a preserved monument to the ancient past. If your work destroys even a small portion of the Spires, you will be subject to the Monument Protection Arm of the Unified Governments of Amnthra...

All of that, followed by legal codes, and legal language. The upshot—years in an Amnthran prison or something equivalent in other parts of the sector, her ship's license removed, and her travel privileges permanently suspended. Even if she didn't get the prison sentence, the other items terrified her more.

She stopped using the sensor. It hadn't compiled any information from the nearby mountains either. They had come up blank on her data screen, which was odd. As if they were simply a holographic feature of the land, something she knew was not true.

She had experienced sensor whiteout on other jobs. Usually the sensors stopped functioning because of a protective field, but she couldn't believe one existed so close to the Spires.

Although something had to exist, given the way her own beam had come back to her, along with a message.

But she hadn't traced that message. It could have come from any part of Amnthra, activated when her sensor touched the protective barrier near the Spires.

She would figure all of that out when she needed to. Right now, she was trying to customize one of the holomaps of the mountain range when her assistant, Roye Bruget, came into the room.

It wasn't really fair to call Roye an assistant. He was more like a part of her. They had worked together from her very first job, and he had saved her butt more times than she wanted to think about.

Sometimes she felt that even though she was nominally in charge, Roye knew more about the way everything worked. Her team usually trusted him to be the voice of reason on all of her jobs. She could be snappish, short, and difficult on good days. Roye was always cheerful, always willing to help.

Unless someone made him angry.

He was a slight, precise man. He wore casual clothes—a shirt and light pants with some slipper-like shoes. The clothes themselves looked pressed, and his hair was so manicured it looked like it had been glued to his head.

"You might want to see this," he said without greeting her.

He moved in front of her to the in-room control panel. He saved her work, moved the holomap to one side, and then did some light touchwork on the panel.

She looked at the translation running across the screen in front of her.

"You broke the Scholars' encryption," she said.

"This wasn't Scholars," he said. "It came from outside their system. The request is direct from the folks in the City of Denon."

She read the request twice. Her heart was pounding. "They want divers?"

"Not any divers," he said. "Cave divers."

"You're sure this isn't a translation error?" she asked. "They don't want spelunkers? They want divers? People who'll go into water in darkness, in caves?"

"Divers," he said.

She let out a small breath. This opened up a wealth of possibilities.

It meant that caves and water existed below the ancient city. Maybe a river. Which would explain how the ancients lived there through countless sieges without massive deaths.

It also gave her a lot of opportunities. If she had the right equipment, she might be able to map the caves using sensors on the ground.

The Unified Government of Amnthra expected sensors from above, but did they expect them from ground level? Probably not.

And then there was the other possibility.

She looked at Roye, her eyes shining. "Did you bring our diving equipment?"

He grinned. "I'm prepared for any emergency, my friend."

She grinned in response.

"This isn't an emergency, Roye," she said. "This is an opportunity."

"One of the best we've ever had," he said.

8

MEKLOS SAT ON THE HARD FLOOR OF HIS TENT. THE TENT was elaborate—nicer, in fact, than the way the academics were living in the city below. His tent had three separate rooms—the main room, where he was now and where he often held meetings; a smaller room to the side that he used as a bedroom; and a fully functional bathroom, complete with sonic or water shower depending on the conditions on the ground.

He had opted for a sonic shower, since it looked like water was scarce here. But no one on the academic team acted like water was scarce, so he might have to reassess that opinion.

He had sent Phineas to get maps from Dr. Reese's assistant, and to remain until he had the latest maps of all the areas, complete with the listings of treasures and protected items. Meklos had a hunch Phin might be gone for a while.

Meklos knew that Dr. Reese was holding something back from him. He just couldn't figure out what it was.

At least she had finally told him what she needed.

She needed protection against thieves, just like he had suspected. Now that the city of Denon was mostly dug out, the academics would set about finding the valuable items, marking them, and figuring out what to do with them.

Amnthra had no laws protecting individual artifacts, meaning the kind that could be moved from one place to another. The Monuments Protection Arm of the Unified Governments of Amnthra hadn't been formed that long ago, and so far, it only applied to things that were defined as part of the land of Amnthra.

The Monuments Protection Arm legislation did specifically mention the Spires of Denon and the City of Denon as protected. But, the word "city" wasn't really defined, and that already presented a problem, at least to Meklos.

Because the definition of city in most Amnthran languages was the same as it was in Meklos's language—a densely populated center.

Which meant that the City of Denon wasn't a city at all by Amnthra's definition. If someone tried to get picky about the legal definitions, he had a hunch they would be able to argue that the City of Denon, as a location, was protected, but movable items within that city, like paintings or jewelry, were not. Even that marvelous inlay floor he had walked across that morning didn't belong to the city.

Because if the floor were removed, the city would remain.

He needed a definition because he needed to know what could remain in this part of Amnthra and what could be removed. He documented everything—his assumptions, his ideas, and his worries—in case Dr. Reese or, worse, the Scholars disagreed with him.

If they disagreed with him, it would probably mean that he had let someone walk off with a part of the city proper.

At least he hoped that was what it would mean. Because the other option was that he had to protect the City from the academics themselves.

Dr. Reese had finally conceded that some of the academics couldn't be trusted. The interns, the post-docs, the guest experts—anyone who wasn't part of her initial team—had to be searched coming in and going out of the area.

As for her initial team, she said she would consider searching them as well, but that sounded dismissive, as if she hoped Meklos would forget he had asked.

He wouldn't forget.

Dr. Reese would soon learn that Meklos rarely forgot anything.

9

GABRIELLE HAD FINALLY FINISHED LAYING OUT THE temple. She had marked off areas, and set up shifts so that the interns (at least the well-trained ones) could begin cleaning off artifacts.

She knew which artifacts she wanted out of the City first. Not the most valuable ones—she would save those until later. First, she wanted some tiny but valuable objects to go to the Scholars, with the message that yes, there was more, and no, she really didn't care which institutions got what pieces.

In truth, she did care, which was why she was sending the less valuable items. However, most of her team did not know which items were extremely valuable and which weren't. Certain items, like statues in one of the houses not far from here, were too big to carry out, at least at the moment.

She was sitting on the temple steps, drinking purified water. The water had a chalky taste that no amount of filtering or purification could get rid of. The water had come from the caverns below. She had known that the ground water was safe to drink since they'd discovered a small spring not far from the city itself.

But the discovery of the larger caverns made her feel even better about drinking the water. Now she knew there was enough to support her people for a long time to come, she had no qualms about using the recycled water for showers and artifact cleansing.

The sun had reached its zenith. She'd learned to recognize it by the way the light fell around the temple. Actually, the light didn't fall as much as it blazed. The entire area became so bright that she actually wore extra eye protection out here.

Even then the brightness was the most amazing thing she'd ever seen. The Spires reflected the sun in all directions, acting like some kind of beacon, sending light cascading down the white part of the mountainside. Then the light hit the white buildings, which reflected it all back to the Spires.

She first experienced the blazing whiteness after the tops of the first buildings were uncovered. She had cleaned the tops, just to see what the original buildings looked like.

Then the sun reached its zenith, the Spires flared and the light cascaded down. She felt as if she were inside a sunlight machine. Her skin—her assistants' skin, everyone's skin—burned. They'd had to put the dirt back on the buildings until they figured out how to deal with the flare of whiteness.

Now, years later, she was no longer frightened of the light and its power. Now, she sat outside and ate her mid-afternoon snack, watching the light reflect, bounce, and reflect again.

The light was her favorite part of this dig—indeed, her favorite part of any dig—and ironically enough (at least to her) she couldn't take with her. This light phenomenon would remain part of Amnthra forever.

She sighed and turned her face upwards. She had skin protectors now, as well as the eye protections. Still, she believed that there was an addictive aspect to the light. When she spent a few of her days in the caves below, she had had a palpable mood shift, one that didn't get corrected until an afternoon in the light bath.

Sometimes that feeling of addiction worried her, made her wonder if she could survive away from this place.

Fortunately, that problem was far in her future. She had so much work to do here that she doubted she'd leave for a long time.

"Gabrielle?"

Yusef.

She tilted her face away from the Spires, blinked several times to clear her eyes, and then looked at him.

He handed her a small communications pad, but her eyes were so sun-blinded that she couldn't see the screen.

Or maybe it just wasn't visible in this light.

She handed it back to him. "I can't see it."

"Come inside." He climbed up the stairs to the inside of the temple.

She sighed, glanced up at the Spires, and watched the shifting light for just a moment. Then she stood—slowly, she'd learned not to stand quickly after a light bath—and went into the temple.

It was at least fifteen degrees cooler inside, maybe more. The dim light, which seemed perfect when she was working here, seemed like the dark of night after the light bath.

She stood in place until her eyes adjusted.

"What is it?" she asked as she took the pad.

"We have divers," he said. "If we want them."

His voice had that odd tone again. She frowned, then tapped the screen. The notification had come back in her personal code: two cave divers nearby, willing to work for a lower price than she had expected, so long as their expenses and insurance costs got met.

"They're not bonded," he said, "and they're not on any approved list of divers. But they're the closest."

"Did you vet them?" she asked.

He nodded. He'd clearly been working in the old Command Center at the base of the mountain rather than with the communications equipment here. The equipment in the city itself wasn't that powerful, and wouldn't have allowed much more than a quick search of nearby archives.

"They seem clean enough. Their records go way back," he said.

"But?"

"No real references," he said.

She clutched the pad. The guards wouldn't like the lack of references.

Or, more clearly, that Meklos Verr wouldn't like it.

But she wasn't working for him. He was working for her.

"I'm not sure it matters," she said. "We need them to see how deep the water runs, if there are any artifacts in the caverns underwater, and where the water actually came from—if they can find that. What else?"

"Nothing," Yusef said.

"They wouldn't even really know what they're seeing, right?" Her heart was pounding. She and Yusef had had only had a handful of conversations like this one over the years. The conversations made her uncomfortable, but they'd been necessary.

"Not if we do it right, no, they wouldn't," he said.

"And if they reported only to us….?"

"Then we should be all right," he said.

She bit her lower lip. The second time that day. She was more nervous than she realized.

"And if we're not all right," Yusef said, "then we…I don't know…"

"It's a risk," she said. "We're hiring them for risky work. Can we afford the insurance payout if it fails?"

He blanched. He always blanched when she asked questions like this.

"Only if it's a one-time payout," he whispered.

No injuries, then. Nothing that would last or linger.

"Do they have families?" she asked.

"Not according to the records. But lots of people in odd jobs never record their families. They're usually running from their families."

"Check on that," she said. "Because if there are no families, then there's probably no one to even pay the insurance to if something goes wrong."

She nodded. "If they have no obvious families, then I think we take the risk. Just you and I. You do know something about diving equipment, right?"

"Enough," he said. His voice shook.

She stared at him. He stared back. Sixteen times they'd had this conversation. Sixteen. And out of those sixteen times, they'd only had to take the hard action four times.

No one else knew.

No one else could know.

"What about Meklos Verr?" she asked. "Will the security team get in the way?"

"Have you told them about the caves?" Yusef asked.

She shook her head.

"You have to," he said.

"No, I don't," she said. "I'm just going to tell them we've found water, and we need to make sure that it's not undermining the city."

"The guy in charge seems smart. He'll know you're lying."

"Only if you tell him," she said. "No one else has been in the caves."

Yusef sighed. "Then I guess we have to keep it that way, don't we?"

"At least for a while," she said.

10

THEY LANDED THEIR AIR-TO-GROUND DEEP EXPLORATION
ship on the far side of Denon's Secret, far away from the
sanctioned trails that wound their way up the mountainside. Even though the ship was in a forest of some kind,
she still had the pilot camouflage the ship.

She didn't want anything to go wrong.

Because of that, she hadn't brought Zeigler, even
though he had begged.

Shortly after the ship arrived, Navi ran the scanning
equipment. If the Unified Governments of Amnthra had
some kind of law against scanning from the ground near
the Spires of Denon, she wanted to be the one who broke
it. She could argue necessity and flash her credentials.

By the time the Unified Governments figured out that
she was subject to the same rules as everyone else, she'd
be long gone.

But she hadn't gotten a notice about the scan, like she
did when they tried to scan Denon's Secret from above.

The scan worked.

She found caves.

The images on her screen looked familiar—a tangle just like Zeigler predicted. She bet if she put a two-dimensional image of the Spires of Denon on top of the image before her, one part of it would match.

She didn't have time for that. She had to find exits from the City of Denon that didn't show up on any modern map.

So far, it looked like this side of the mountain had about two dozen of them.

11

It had taken Meklos two days to figure out the best way to deploy his team.

Fifteen wasn't enough. Fifteen wasn't close to enough. If he ran long shifts, he only had seven actual humans on the ground. He and Phineas had to monitor the robots and the various detectors. Since he and Phin were on opposite shifts, they wouldn't see each other except when they relieved each other.

He didn't like that set-up at all. Usually he and Phin coordinated and put an able but less important team member on the equipment.

He had already sent for reinforcements.

They wouldn't come for a week. He'd stressed the urgency, but he couldn't name the threat, so he knew he went into the queue behind some less important but more easily definable jobs.

And now, Dr. Reese had thrown him another curve. She had hired two new experts to come into the city. She wouldn't define their area of expertise, nor would she let him vet them.

They're my responsibility, Meklos, she'd said in that snotty tone of hers, and no matter how much he argued, he couldn't convince her otherwise.

So he was going to meet them near the old Command Center at the base of the mountain.

Instead of pulling one of his seven-member team off recon, he woke Phin just before heading to the Command Center. He also took two members of Phin's team with him down the mountainside. They would set up as if they were guarding the Command Center.

When Meklos had asked to accompany Chavo to the newcomers' ship, Dr. Reese had denied his request.

I need to see exactly what they're flying and where it came from, Meklos said.

They're vetted, Dr. Reese said. *And besides, you'll escort them into the city and out of the city. They won't be able to do anything.*

Little did she know. He'd seen a single person disrupt one of the most orderly jobs he'd had. That person had destroyed everything in a short period of time.

So he pulled rank on Dr. Reese again, and told her that he would inspect the newcomers' equipment and supplies. What he didn't tell her was that he would take their names and any other identifying information and vet them himself.

Meklos had sent Valma Tanis to the old Command Center ahead of him. He and Declan Ceema, who had been with him almost since Meklos began security work, climbed down the mountainside together.

Going down was considerably harder than coming up. He hadn't quite realized how steep the grade was. Fortunately, his hands were free. He carried his usual weapons—a laser pistol (even though they were banned near the Spires), a knife, and a small explosive charge that he didn't dare use near the top of the mountain. All of those were hidden away on his person. Most people wouldn't be able to see the weapons at all, just his small comm unit, attached to his hip.

Declan had similar weapons, although not the explosive, since Meklos didn't want a member of his team forgetting where they were and accidentally causing damage to the Spires.

The old Command Center had been the original base for the first Scholars team to come to Denon's Secret. The team arrived shortly after some members of a mountain climbing expedition realized that the Spires weren't some kind of natural phenomenon.

Initial Scholars teams were so well funded that they always built a command and control center. The center had sleeping quarters, a fully stocked kitchen, indoor plumbing, and a communications array that rivaled the ones on many ships.

The building itself was located below the lines that the Monuments Protection Arm had designated to protect the Spires. He suspected the line was designed to exclude the Command Center, since it predated not only the line, but the Monuments Protection Arm as well.

He appreciated the lack of designation—because it meant that he could use the communications equipment without worrying about damaging the Spires. He suspected he would have a lot of work to do here, even after he had vetted the newcomers.

His other team member waited outside the Command Center's main door. Valma Tanis was a tall woman. She wore shorts and a t-shirt that bared her muscular arms despite the sunburn threat. Long ago, she had led a military unit stationed on a planet hotter and brighter than this one; the implants she got as part of that service would allow her to stand in light two times brighter than this without any noticeable skin damage.

"Any sign of them?" Meklos asked.

The center itself stood in the exact middle of the path that Chavo and the two newcomers would take to come up the mountainside.

"Not yet," Valma said. "I checked for ships. They have a single space cruiser parked in the designated zone. The ship is small and had to have come from a relatively short distance away."

"How short?" Meklos asked.

"The nearest star base is about the extent of its range."

He felt a surge of irritation. If Dr. Reese had told him more about these two, he wouldn't worry about such things as ships and ranges and travel times.

"Any identifying marks?" he asked.

"Just commercial ones. The ship was purchased from a regular dealer, without any government or business labels. It's not connected to the Scholars, and it's not part of any known business."

Which could be good and bad. If they weren't affiliated, then they had no real contacts, and couldn't be expected to have any kind of backup. Or the ship looked deliberately innocuous, to make anyone who wanted to check on it relax their guard.

"Ships in orbit?" he asked.

"More than I care to count," she said. "This center doesn't have the equipment to surreptitiously scan them, but I did check with the Unified Governments, and they say nothing out of the ordinary is going on up there."

Well, that was something, at least. He gazed down the trail. It was quite a hike from the designated parking area, and if the two newcomers didn't know how to pack, they'd be struggling by the time they got here.

Declan came round the building. He was short and squat, stronger than he looked and older as well. His fatigues were covered with the red dust from this lower section of the mountain.

"They're winding their way around the last part of the trail," he said. "Chavo, a man, and a woman. They have professional-level backpacks."

"Any idea who they are?" Meklos asked.

"I can go inside, scan, and see if I get identifiers," Declan said.

Meklos shook his head. He could see them now, both taller than the too-thin Chavo. "There isn't time."

He turned to Valma.

"Get them water," he said.

She nodded and disappeared into the command center. He should have thought of that earlier. People were much more willing to subject themselves to search when they thought the people searching them were kind.

She came back out with three chilled bottles in her right hand just as Chavo and the other two arrived. Chavo saw Meklos and rolled his eyes. Meklos ignored him.

Meklos stepped forward and extended his hand. "Meklos Verr, head of security."

The woman was the one who took his hand, which meant she was the one in charge.

"Navi Salvino," she said, "and my partner, Roye Bruget."

Meklos nodded at Valma. She handed out the water. Bruget put the bottle against his forehead and closed his eyes. Obviously the heat was getting to him already.

Salvino opened her bottle and took a dainty sip. She seemed fine, but Meklos didn't know if that was an act or not.

"I'm sorry," he said as gently as he could. "I need you to state your purpose here so that I can check it against our logs."

"We're the cave divers that Dr. Reese sent for," Salvino said.

Salvino's words so shocked him that he nearly repeated what she said to make sure he'd heard it correctly. Cave divers? Dr. Reese had said nothing about caves. If caves honeycombed a mountain like Denon's Secret, then they were a security risk, and one he should have known about from the very beginning.

Meklos hoped his shock hadn't shown on his face. He glanced at Chavo who shrugged. Apparently he hadn't known either.

Declan had moved slightly into a more defensive position. Valma watched warily from the side of the path.

"We need to search your packs," Meklos said.

"Sure," Salvino said.

She slid her pack off her shoulders and set it on the ground. Bruget did the same, opening his quickly, then stepping back.

Salvino stepped back as well. They'd clearly been searched many times before.

"We'll need to search you as well," Declan said.

They both nodded.

Valma watched. Meklos had been shot once during a search. He'd been so focused on the search that he forgot to keep an eye on the people whose items he was going through. Ever since, he had three people on a potential search: two to search and one to watch.

The packs were a revelation. He'd worked with water divers before. They always had breathing equipment, some kind of environmental suit, and supplies, but these two also had recording technology, a variety of lights, and special sonar. He didn't see the breathing equipment.

He held up one of the sonar pieces. "You'll have to clear that with Dr. Reese. You might be operating it too close to the Spires."

As he mentioned the Spires, both Salvino and Bruget looked up, their mouths open slightly.

Declan ignored the movement. He continued the hands-on search, then followed it with a full body scan.

"Clean," he said.

Meklos pulled out one of the suits. "This seems more like a space diving suit than a water diving suit."

Salvino nodded. "It's made specially for cave diving," she said. "You can get trapped in a very small space in a cave, and you need to survive, sometimes for a day or more, while you're waiting for your partner to go for help. Which is why, you'll note, we also have an extra suit, in case there are divers above who could assist."

Meklos wasn't sure he believed the explanation. He had done water diving himself, but never with a suit this thin. Suits like this worked best in the vacuum of space. The oxygen was threaded through the material instead of in sturdy containers worn at the hip.

He always thought suits like this dangerous because they could rip so easily, which would disturb the oxygen flow.

Still, he noted the make of the suits, and the design number. He would vet those as well.

Otherwise he found nothing in the packs. He slid them back to their owners for repacking.

The other thing he noticed about the packs was that they had no room for extras. Everything inside had a purpose for this trip, and there was no way any of it could be left behind.

If these two people wanted to smuggle something out of the City of Denon, then they would have to do it by leaving all of their equipment behind.

"Okay," he said after catching Declan's nod. "You're ready to go up. Declan and Valma will join you. Chavo here will give you both the speech about the Spires as you climb. If you need more water, say so now. It'll only get hotter the higher we go."

Neither Salvino nor Bruget looked surprised when he said that, which bothered him. He had been surprised about the warmth up top, and he had researched the Naramzin Mountain Range as well as the Spires.

Maybe their research was more thorough.

Or maybe they weren't just experts in cave diving. Maybe they were experts in something else as well.

He hoped he would have enough time to find out.

12

Navi climbed slowly, pretending she wasn't familiar with the path. In truth, she'd studied it for nearly a week. The path and the Spires and the ground around it all, as well as the designated areas.

She also had a complete map of the caverns, made with her scanning equipment. The deep exploration ship was where she had left it, with her people inside. They could no longer send her updates, but she didn't need them. Unless there were cave-ins or some serious problems (and, honestly, wouldn't the cave-ins have shown up in the scan?), all they had to do was wait for her all-clear.

She could finally understand why Zeigler had fallen in love with this place. The light alone was refreshing, even though it was amazingly bright. The Spires were spectacular. She was actually excited about seeing the city.

The diving worried her—she hadn't done anything like that in a long time—but it would end quickly. She had lied about the timing to that security guard. These caverns and passageways were too honeycombed to get lost in for long.

As long as she had a partner and as long as they were vigilant about going one at a time, only one could get trapped. And they had the equipment to get that person out, which the guard hadn't really said anything about.

Maybe he hadn't noticed.

More likely, her ruse was working.

She wasn't sure how long it would. That guard looked smarter than she liked. And while all of the information she had set up on nearby databases about her cave diving experience was true, it wasn't complete. She had left off dates and travel times because they were too far apart for a professional cave diver.

Someone smart might also realize that most of her cave diving experience was near archeological digs like this one. She'd tried to cover it in the bio she'd created—saying that she specialized in diving digs, but she wasn't sure that was enough.

And since she'd used her own name, there was always the possibility that someone who dug deep enough might find out how she really made her living.

Then she'd be in trouble.

But she wasn't going to think about that. She was going in, she was going to inspect the site, she would do her dive, and she would leave.

After that, she would decide what to do next.

13

THE INFORMATION ON THE CAVE DIVERS WAS CLEAN, BUT sparse. Meklos didn't like sparse. It was his experience that sparse was rare. In general, there was too much information on most people, and even more on most businesses.

Meklos was hunched over the control board, looking at an actual screen. The command center was quiet. He was alone in here.

He hadn't worked on equipment this old in quite a while. He hated how slow the information flow was. He had a limited amount of time, and the system itself was holding him back.

The fact that he could only find the necessary information on the cave divers made him suspicious. It seemed like information had been removed from their bios.

He could always find added information. Added information announced itself, often by being in the wrong place. Added information also had the wrong or misleading dates, or dates that didn't somehow jibe with other dates already in the biographical information.

But when information was removed, the gaps weren't as obvious. The gaps could simply be that: gaps. It would take time he didn't have to prove that the missing information was somehow important.

He would have done all of that if he had been consulted *before* Dr. Reese hired these people. But he was brought in afterwards, and not asked to double-check them.

If Dr. Reese had problems with her cave divers, those problems would be her own fault. He had to file a report for Scholars—the standard weekly update—and he would note the lack of consultation.

He would also remark that, even though Dr. Reese had requested a security team, she didn't really seem to want one. She certainly wasn't working with him, and that made his job that much harder.

He would also make note of the caves.

He sighed. One reason he couldn't properly vet the cave divers was that he wanted to see what he could find on the caves. He had a hunch that Dr. Reese would lie to him about them.

So far as he could tell, no one knew that caves existed beneath the City of Denon.

Some academic from a college too small to be in the Scholar's system postulated that caves existed beneath the city; he figured it was the only way the ancients could survive all the sieges. He also postulated a river running through those caves as well.

But that was just a hypothesis, not fact.

Meklos figured if Dr. Reese had hired cave divers, she had found caves—and they were filled with water.

He wondered what else she was searching for.

He doubted she would tell him.

He could only hope that he would figure it out before there was any trouble.

But he even doubted that.

14

By the time they'd reached the City of Denon, Navi was exhausted. She was getting too old for this much exercise, particularly in an environment as hostile as this one. The heat was oppressive, the light brighter than anything she could have imagined. Her pack's normal weight seemed too much for her.

Too many months on the ship, doing exercise in artificial gravity, and not enough time planetside. She hoped she didn't show it.

Because she didn't want to be here any longer than she needed to. Infiltration operations went best when they were quick and dirty.

Just coming down the trail, she saw more than she expected. The security team's automatic tents were sophisticated and expensive. This wasn't some low-rent team, but one that obviously came highly recommended.

That made her nervous. She had been right to worry about Verr, the head of security. He clearly had the smarts—and the wherewithal—to break through her information screens.

If he had enough time.

The key was to make sure he didn't have enough time.

She took in as much information as she could. Roye had surreptitiously recorded the Spires, which were so much more impressive in person than they ever could be on any holographic representation.

The city was remarkably well preserved. Parts still hadn't been uncovered yet, of course, and might not be for some time. But the way that the light reflected off the cleansed buildings suggested this place had been amazing in its day.

It was amazing now.

And it was filled with unrecorded treasures. Things that could be sold for unbelievable prices to collectors and never get recorded as stolen.

If Zeigler was right about the caves—that they had once been a museum for war trophies—then the number of unrecorded treasures would increase exponentially.

The little guide, Chavo, had taken them to a small undecorated house at the edge of the city. Navi got the message. There was nothing here for them to steal. In fact, if they weren't that bright and didn't look around, they might think their house representative—that the ancient Denonites preferred unadorned houses and buildings, that the treasure would be the city itself and not the wares housed within.

She knew better.

The Denonites had spread their style throughout this part of the sector. When they conquered a nation, they kept troops onsite until the nation was completely plundered. Sometimes that took decades.

So the Denonites made themselves at home, building houses like this one—on one floor, with one or two bedrooms, a living area, and a nice kitchen. Only every single part of the building had decoration, be it a wall painting or a small flower-decorated cornice or a statue to hide a particularly mundane corner.

Those treasures, in those conquered cities, had been recorded long ago.

It was the heart of the Denonite empire that hadn't been found—until Dr. Gabrielle Reese and her team of scholars stumbled upon the ancient city of Denon itself.

Roye had already made himself at home here. He'd given them both water and some nutrient bars, then slathered oil on his skin. She needed to do the same.

He was studying her as she moved around the house, getting her bearings. Chavo would be back soon to take them to meet Dr. Reese and discuss the job ahead.

Navi hoped Dr. Reese would provide dinner, because the nutrient bars weren't going to hold her for long.

"We can postpone the dive for a day or two," Roye said. "Get our bearings and do this right."

"It's not about the dive," Navi said. "We can't stay here long."

He continued to stare at her. "If we're too tired, we'll make mistakes."

She smiled at him. "The dive'll be safe enough. The suits will protect us."

He shook his head.

"I programmed them with the maps," she said. "The suits'll get us out, even if we're unconscious. Someone will find us. We'll be fine."

"One extra day," he said. "That's all I'm asking."

She thought of that guard's face, the look he had gotten when she mentioned cave diving. Something had happened just behind his eyes, but she wasn't quite sure what it was.

"No," she said. "We dive and then we leave. That's all."

"All right," Roye said, shaking his head. He didn't have to add that he disagreed with her.

She already knew.

15

"When were you going to tell me about the caves?"

Gabrielle jumped. She thought she was alone in the temple. She was testing her new system, placing items in their designated areas. Then she had gone to the back and cleaned a small elaborate vase.

She was just drying off her hands, when Meklos interrupted her.

He was standing just outside her work area, hands on his hips, his shirt covered in sweat. His boots had left a mixture of white and red dust on the image of the Spires, dust that glommed together wherever his sweat dripped onto it.

"You're making a mess," she said.

She continued drying her hands so that he couldn't see how they were shaking. She hadn't expected him to confront her about this. She had already told him she was hiring experts. He shouldn't have questioned them.

Her word should have been enough.

"Caves," he said. "Tell me about the caves."

She shrugged. "There's not much to tell. They're caves."

"If they're just caves, why did you hire divers?" he asked.

She sighed. She wanted him to feel her exasperation so that he wouldn't ask too many more questions.

"Because," she said, "the caves are full of water. I want to see if that water comes from a natural stream or if it is something that will undermine the entire city. That's somewhat important."

"More important than you know," he said, "since caves have branches, and they're not always logical."

"So?" she asked.

"So people can either enter and leave this city through caves. Or haven't you thought of that?"

She didn't like his tone. And, if she were honest with herself, she would have to admit she didn't like him.

Hiring the guards had been a mistake. She should have done so long after she knew exactly what kind of treasures she had. And then she should have hired some kind of escort, not someone to guard the city itself.

"They can't get in and out," she said slowly, as if he were a particularly stupid child. "The caves are full of water."

"I would like to see them," he said.

"Well, so would I," she said, "but I'm not qualified to dive them. Are you?"

He glared at her. "Your experts have thin résumés."

He didn't exactly answer her, which she did not appreciate.

"And your resume is a little too thick," she said. "We really don't need this level of security."

He stared at her for a moment. He looked as exasperated as she felt.

"All right," he said finally. "Hire someone else—someone who'll stand where you tell them to and march where you want them to and look the other way when you ask them to. When that group arrives, we'll leave. Okay?"

It was what she wanted. It was what she needed. If she could figure out how, she'd ask him and his team to leave immediately.

But she was the one who had conjured up the threat. She was the one who would have to live with this horribly overexperienced security team until someone better arrived.

"Yes," she said. "I think that would be for the best."

16

THE CAVERN WAS UNBELIEVABLY COLD. NAVI HAD NOTICED that the night before, and thought it simply the contrast between her overheated body and the natural chill any underground area had. But this chill was deeper than that.

It made her relieved she had a space-equipped suit, one that could handle extreme cold with ease. Still, it was the thought of going into the cold, especially when she was so tired from the heat, that made her nervous.

The cavern looked the same as it had the night before. Gabrielle Reese and her assistant had put lights everywhere, making passage down easy. As Navi walked with her equipment, she noted niches in the wall, but she didn't have time to look at them closely.

Neither did Roye. Nor could they show a lot of interest in the niches. Because they were here to see what was in the water, whether there were more caverns and maybe an underground river or, Gabrielle Reese had said disingenuously, "a settlement."

She hadn't mentioned a museum or artifacts.

But it seemed to Navi, just from the niches alone, that Zeigler's idea of a museum was a good one. If the niches were manmade—and she guessed from their positions that they were—then they had once held items.

She couldn't get close enough to see if the items were recently removed. There would be markings in the dirt if they were.

She and Roye hadn't discussed this much the night before, in case they were overheard. But they did confirm the plan with a sort of shorthand.

If they found nothing in the water except more caverns or the source of the water itself, then they would surface in the cavern and report directly to Gabrielle Reese as they (supposedly) were being paid to do.

But if they found artifacts or evidence of another city, they would go out the passageways and return to the camouflaged ship.

It sounded simple. But the dive happened between those two choices.

Now she wished she hadn't been quite so impetuous.

Now she wished she had hired someone else to go into the murky deep.

17

THE CAVERNS WERE EMPTY AND THERE WERE MORE OF them than Meklos realized. Dr. Reese had told him that there were only a few caves—not these vast cathedral-like spaces that could house hundreds, maybe thousands, of people.

She wasn't happy that he had come with the divers. But he wanted to watch them suit up. He also didn't like the half-empty packs, the way that they glanced at each other, as if confirming some pre-arranged signal.

He hadn't had his team bring diving equipment on this mission, so he couldn't send someone with the divers. He wouldn't be able to monitor them, since the scanning requirements near the Spires were so restrictive.

He was glad he had sent the weekly update from the Command Center. When the Scholars saw that in conjunction with the news that Dr. Reese had let the team go, they would understand why.

And maybe they would send someone to supervise Dr. Reese.

It took three crumbling flights of stairs—maybe as old as the Spires—to get to the cavern with the water. The water was a chalky mess of dust and some kind of oil.

He wouldn't want to go into it, although he gathered, from Dr. Reese's conversation with the divers, that she had waded into it more than once.

He couldn't imagine why. She wouldn't know where to put her feet or what she was stepping on. She also couldn't know if there was a current.

Because if this was part of a river, there could be a very strong current, one that might take divers and force them away from the caverns altogether.

He mentioned this to the woman, Salvino. She had nodded, looking a little distracted. The man, Bruget, was the one who answered.

"The suits are state of the art. They can keep us alive in adverse conditions for days. By then, we should figure out where we are and how to get out."

"Unless there is only one way out," Meklos said.

"Even then," Bruget said. "A lead, a line…."

"Or a small explosive," Salvino said.

"…would get us out."

An explosive. As if Dr. Reese would allow one to go off below the city.

Still, Meklos had made his protest—both to them and to Dr. Reese. He had done what he could.

They were professionals. Theoretically, they knew what they were getting into.

The water started as a small trickle at the edge of this cavern. If Dr. Reese was right, the water level had been rising for centuries.

But, she added, no one knew that for certain. For all they knew, the caverns got flooded five hundred years ago and the water was evaporating.

The divers were to find the source, if they could. If they couldn't, they were to go all the way to the bottom of the caverns.

Salvino warned that the dives might take days. She promised that they wouldn't stay under more than five hours each, and she recommended someone stay in the cavern at all times.

Dr. Reese's assistant, Yusef Kimber, would wait down here during this first dive. Apparently Dr. Reese didn't want the non-permanent members of her team to even know the caverns were here—someone like Chavo or the other students.

That alone made Meklos suspicious.

Normally, watching over a dive was the kind of crappy mindless job given to someone with no status whatsoever.

The divers set down their packs on a flat area not too far from the water's edge. They opened the packs in unison, and removed their suits.

Meklos had watched divers before. Generally they stripped before suiting up, but these two did not. They slid their suits over their clothing, then with a nod to each other, over their faces.

Hands went up, adjusting, twisting, making certain. At one point, both divers stopped and stared at each other.

They didn't have helmets. The suit itself covered their faces, leaving only their eyes visible.

As they stared at each other, he realized they were checking their communications equipment.

He wondered if Dr. Reese realized that, and if she did, if she objected to the use of the equipment. He didn't know how far its reach was, but it had to cover a good distance, in case the divers got separated.

He glanced at Dr. Reese. She watched intently, her fingers threaded together. As the divers continued to check their equipment, she twisted her fingers, keeping them locked, but trying to pull them apart at the same time.

She was nervous, almost frightened.

Finally, the divers finished. They turned to Meklos and Dr. Reese. The divers were distinguishable now only by height and body shape. The suits themselves matched. The suits looked like a thin silver coating that someone had applied over every centimeter of the divers. The suits moved easily with the divers.

After a moment, the divers gave Dr. Reese a tiny salute. Then Salvino walked into the water, followed closely by Bruget. It took them only a few steps to disappear.

"Do you have some kind of communicator to stay in touch with them?" Meklos asked.

Dr. Reese shook her head. "We can't use equipment that powerful here," she said. "Although we did compromise and let them bring their emergency beacons. If they get in trouble, we'll know, and we'll know where to find them."

"Then what?" Meklos asked. "We don't have another diver."

"We'll figure it out if it happens," she said. "I doubt that it will."

He shivered, a movement that had nothing to do with the cold. He loathed her callousness, and her blithe assumption that everything would be fine.

No one knew what was down there. No one knew what they would encounter.

And whenever anyone was in a situation where no one knew what could go wrong, something inevitably did.

"I hope you're insured if something goes wrong here," he said.

She glanced at him.

"I have no idea," she said. Then she smiled. "But I do know that they are."

18

THE WATER WAS COLD. NAVI COULDN'T FEEL IT THROUGH her suit, but she knew it anyway, and that made her shiver. The whole dive was making her nervous, in a way that she didn't entirely understand.

The final equipment check worked. The comm was on. She walked down into the submerged cavern, the water rising until it covered her head.

The water was chalky, murky, dark, like a lake after someone had disturbed the sediment below. She turned on the suit's dim lights—which Roye called fog lights—and could see a bit better.

Then she turned on all of her cameras. She wanted this dive recorded, so she wouldn't have to repeat it.

If they found something, she wanted to be able to identify it clearly.

You back there? she asked Roye through the comm.

Right behind you, he said.

His voice sounded small and mechanical through the suit. She fought the urge to turn toward him.

Deploy map, she said.

She hadn't dared give that order above in case they were monitoring the communication. But she doubted they would monitor through the water.

Gabrielle Reese didn't even seem to care about communications. She seemed detached, almost withdrawn. When Roye had brought up the idea of a malfunction, she had shrugged.

She really didn't seem to care if they survived or not.

That was one way to run a dig. It didn't matter how many people died, just so long as the artifacts got out.

But Navi had checked before she even arrived on Amnthra. Gabrielle Reese's digs suffered no more deaths than other digs. No more, but no less either. She always seemed to stay within the average, even though her earlier digs were on worlds much more hostile than this one.

The only anomaly in any of the information was that Gabrielle Reese's digs often had deaths later rather than earlier.

Navi could find no reason for that little statistical blip. Although now, as she walked along the bottom of this cavern in the murky darkness, she wondered if it wasn't because Dr. Reese ceased using precautions later in her projects—precautions that were in place early on.

Navi turned on her map. It rose in front of her left eye. The map itself was a series of thin outlines, clear so that she could see through them. Except for the red dot which marked where she was standing, she saw no color at all.

There's a lot of cave to go, she said.

But not a lot of cavern, Roye said. *We explore this area here, and that's about it. If we're going to find anything, it'll be here.*

She turned on the lights above her helmet and in her fingertips. She directed the beams toward the walls.

More little niches, but they appeared empty.

She would have to get closer to make sure.

Sediment did flow around her, like snow in a harsh breeze. The water was hard to walk through, but she didn't want to swim. She wasn't sure it would be easier—the water seemed more viscous here than it had on the surface.

What the hell is this stuff? she asked.

Taking a sample now, he said. *It's got some chemical composition that wasn't present above, but if we want a better reading we're going to need the ship's equipment.*

Just great, she said, but she kept walking.

Finally, she reached the wall. Niches stacked on top of each other like cubbyholes. Gingerly she eased her left hand inside, and found nothing. The edges of the niche were waterworn, and the walls themselves seemed furry.

Mold maybe, or some kind of algae. She took a sample of that and placed it in her own kit.

Whatever that stuff was, it meant that this part of the cavern had been underwater for a very long time.

This seems a little weird to be a museum, Roye said.

Let's not jump to conclusions, she said. *We're just getting started.*

Then she shivered again. They were just getting started. They had planned their route the night before: This series of large caverns, then two passageways down, another bigger cave. If they didn't find anything there, they'd use scanning equipment to see if they could find the water's source.

And if they didn't find that, then they would work their way back.

She was ready to go back now. She was so tense that she had been grinding her teeth—at least, she thought she had. They ached, even though her jaw didn't.

You finding anything? she asked Roye.

A whole lotta nothing, he said.

Me too. But she dutifully felt and walked and recorded, going over the giant cavern bit by furry bit.

19

THE DIVERS DISAPPEARED UNDER THE WATER. GABRIELLE watched for several minutes, until the bubbles faded and she couldn't see shadows moving under the surface.

The cold had numbed her hands—she hadn't worn gloves or added protection because she knew she wouldn't be down here long.

Besides, she liked carrying the chill to the surface and let the sun burn it off her.

She was about to leave when something rustled behind her. She turned.

Meklos was kneeling in front of the divers' packs. He had opened one and was taking the pieces out.

"I thought you already inspected those," she said.

"I did," he said. "I wanted to see if they added anything."

"You still don't trust them," she said.

"You pay me not to trust anyone."

She shook her head. She was glad he would be gone soon. Who knew that security guards could be so thorough?

She watched him take items out—things she couldn't quite identify. And then he stopped as he removed an extra suit.

"You got someone who can use this?" he asked.

She shook her head. She had no idea. He had asked something similar before, and she hadn't known the answer then either.

She wasn't sure why he cared.

"So they have a backup," she said. "So what?"

"Backup," he muttered. "Hmmm."

He set the suit aside and continued his search.

"If you don't need me any longer," she said, "I'm heading to the surface where it's warm."

Without waiting for his answer, she walked around him to the stairs. She glanced at Yusef. He was bundled in three extra layers of clothing beneath his heavy coat.

"You'll be all right?" she asked.

He held up a reading pad and pointed to his lunch. "I'm here for the long haul."

She smiled at him. Then she took one last look at the water. It seemed completely undisturbed now, as if there weren't two humans beneath it.

A chill ran down her spine. She certainly wouldn't go down there.

But, then, she wasn't being paid to.

20

MEKLOS HAD CLEARED OUT THE PACKS, FINDING NOTHING he hadn't seen before. He wasn't exactly sure what he was looking for—a small piece of equipment, a tiny receiver, something. But he didn't find anything except the third suit.

Was it simply a required precaution or was there a third diver hiding somewhere?

He didn't know enough about professional cave diving to know what the required precautions were. Regular water diving didn't last as long as a cave dive; the suits weren't as sophisticated and weren't meant to last for days should something go wrong.

He picked up the suit and poked it with his finger. It stretched, then embraced his finger, becoming a part of it.

He had a hunch puncturing this thing would take a great deal of work. It might be impossible.

So it wasn't as fragile as it initially seemed.

If the suit had belonged to Dr. Reese, he would have punctured it and dealt with the consequences. But he didn't want to risk insulting the experts.

Besides, they might need that third suit for a reason he hadn't yet thought of. He didn't dare do anything to it, at least until the dive was over.

But he did turn it inside out. Controls were scattered throughout—some on the fingertips, some on the back of the hand. Others ran along the chin.

The eye area was clear, but probably had some kind of communications screen. He pressed one of the control chips along the chin and the eye area lit up. He pressed another and got a temperature readout that ran along the side of the right eye.

Then he pressed a third and the Spires appeared before the left eye, looking just like they did on the floor of the temple.

Only on this image of the Spires was clear, except for the outlines of the branches and a red dot at the edge of one of the wide areas.

His heart started to pound. He picked up the suit and carried it to the steps.

The red dot moved with him.

He cursed.

"Everything okay?" Yusef asked.

Meklos almost cursed again. He had forgotten Yusef was here.

"Yeah," he said. "I accidentally turned something on. I need to figure out how to shut it off."

"Let me." Yusef had to struggle to stand with all of his layers of clothing.

Meklos pressed the controls again. The Spires disappeared.

"Never mind," he said. "I got it."

"Never seen a suit like that before, huh?" Yusef asked.

"Not like this," Meklos said. "Have you?"

"I try not to do anything that requires I carry my environment with me," Yusef said. "This is as close to an environmental suit as I get."

He indicated his coat and boots.

Meklos smiled because he was supposed to. Then he shut off the other parts of the suit, turned it right-side out, and put it back inside the pack.

Then he turned to Yusef. "You sure you don't want one of my team down here too?"

Yusef shrugged. "I'm okay by myself."

"You've established emergency procedures?"

"I have some field medicine training, if needed. Besides, I'm pretty sure they'll be fine. If the caverns below are anything like the caverns up here, there aren't even sharp edges for them to get caught on."

He was as cavalier as his employer. Maybe that was why Yusef and Dr. Reese got along so well.

"I'll be back down before they're due to come up," Meklos said.

"Okay." Yusef sounded like he didn't care. He pressed himself against the wall, getting white residue on the back of his coat. He sank to the floor facing the water, but pulled out his work pad.

Meklos shook his head. Maybe he'd send someone down.

After he had some time to think.

Because he felt mildly stupid already. How could he have missed it? The Spires weren't some artistic design. They were a map.

A three-dimensional map of the cave system below the city.

But why would there be a map of the caves so visible from the mountaintop?

"You guys ever figure out what the Spires were for?" Meklos asked.

Yusef gave him an annoyed look. Clearly the man wanted to be left alone. "They were never my specialty. I came here for the city."

"But has anyone figured out what they're for? I mean, they're pretty dramatic."

"The whole place is dramatic," Yusef said.

Meklos stared at him.

Yusef figured out that he wasn't going to leave until the question got answered.

"And no, no one knows for certain what they are. All that inlay, all that writing, the way they vibrate if you hit them too hard says artwork to me. But I'll leave it to people who are interested. I'd much rather look at a building than some sculpture that people attached to a mountaintop."

He sounded convinced. He sounded irritated.

Meklos nodded. "Thanks," he said. "I was just wondering."

"Yep," Yusef said. "Everyone wonders about this place. Maybe someday we'll have answers."

"Maybe," Meklos said as he mounted the stairs for the surface.

And maybe, he thought, *some people already had this place all figured out.*

21

NOTHING IN THE WIDEST PART OF THE CAVERNS. NAVI had steeled herself to come across some statue, a face looming in the murk, maybe, or an arm reaching out to her.

But nothing like that happened.

She walked through meters and meters of thick water, the white sediment thick and flowing around her as if she were in the middle of a blizzard.

Creepiest dive I've done in a long time, Roye said.

Me, too.

She had been hoping for artifacts. Maybe they got moved as the caverns flooded. Maybe she would step into one of the smaller areas and find everything crammed against the walls, forced by the force of the water.

You don't think this white stuff is from dissolved artifacts, do you? she asked.

No, he said. *Haven't you noticed? The walls flake.*

I thought that was algae.

It is—or something like it—in the niches. But the walls themselves. Touch one. You'll see.

She was close to an outcropping. She touched its rounded surface gently. As her fingers found the surface, a flurry of white chips entered the water and flowed with it.

There is some kind of current down here, isn't there? she asked.

I'm not sure, he said. *We could be doing this. I'm not getting readings that suggest anything other than our disturbing the environment.*

She wasn't either. She just wanted to find something.

She moved into the next cavern. It seemed darker than the one before, even though she knew that wasn't possible.

No light filtered down here except the lights she and Roye had brought with them.

At least the water hadn't gotten any thicker. She glanced at the map. One more large room to go after this one. Then the passageways.

Then she could get out.

This would be her last cave dive. If she ever had to go through a ruse like this again, she would stay on the surface and supervise. They would bring a new cave diver in.

She was getting too old and too impatient for this kind of thing.

Or maybe the impatience was coming from the lack of treasure.

She loved treasure just like everyone else.

The only difference was all she had to do was touch it. Then it was hers forever.

22

MEKLOS HADN'T REALIZED HOW COLD HE HAD BECOME in that cavern. His hands ached. His nose throbbed. The moment the sunlight hit him, the blood rose in his skin, attempting to warm him.

How cold had it been down there?

Colder than it should have been, even in an underground chamber.

He wondered what caused that.

Those caverns were important in a way he couldn't understand. And if Yusef's comments were to be believed, Dr. Reese and her team didn't understand either.

They didn't even realize that the Spires were a map.

Meklos moved away from the building that housed the entrance to the caverns. He stepped into an open area and looked up.

He had been right.

The image he had seen in that suit was the Spires, with a dot indicating where he was.

A map.

And his little cave divers, the experts who supposedly knew nothing about this dig, had known about that.

What else did they know?

He really should have gone to Dr. Reese and told her that her experts knew more about this place than she did, but he wasn't going to—at least not yet.

The walk across the city of Denon took longer than he expected it to. He didn't walk along the main roads, but stayed to the backs of buildings.

Not everything was excavated yet. He had to go around mounds of reddish brown dirt, some of which had reattached itself to nearby white buildings.

Only the larger buildings had been completely excavated. The smaller ones were still half buried.

He hadn't realized that before. He'd never done a thorough walk-through of the city. He'd been too busy setting up defensive parameters, and trying to find out exactly what Dr. Reese wanted and then worrying about these so-called experts.

He hadn't had time to do some of the most important work at this job.

But he had had a chance to examine the building where they housed the cave divers. He hadn't come at it from this angle before—he'd come at it from the front, off the main road, which was where it was situated.

Coming from the back and side, he realized that half the buildings behind it weren't fully excavated. Their basic shape had been dug out, and many had been excavated down to the foundation on one side only—usually the side that faced the main street.

Someone could have—and probably had—gone inside, looked around, and then gone back out. But dirt remained on the walls, and seemed to fill the back areas.

Oddly enough, however, the roofs on all of the buildings had been cleaned off. They were that same pristine white as the excavated parts of the city.

He didn't think about the reasons for that—although he did know the effect. It maximized the light and the reflections.

This place was already overly bright. Clearing the roofs of all the buildings made it even brighter.

He ducked inside the building that had housed the cave divers and had to blink at the darkness. Even now, his eyes had trouble adjusting to the shift in light levels.

He had to pause and wait for his eyes to adjust, which annoyed him. If someone wanted to attack him here, all they had to do was wait until he came in from the outside.

Fortunately, no one lurked inside. The main room barely looked used, and the air mattresses in the back were pressed against the wall, like beds on a ship, their covers folded and pristine as if they were newly made.

The cave divers hadn't left many of their belongings. The clothes they wore the day before were hanging off one of two chairs that Dr. Reese had provided. A few personal items were scattered on the only table.

A secondary pack, one that had initially been tucked into the other packs, waited near the foot of one of the beds, but had nothing inside.

The emptiness bothered him. The way the couple had described the cave dives had given him the impression that they would be here for several days, taking each dive slowly, especially if they had to look for the water's source.

But the building didn't look like someone planned to camp here for several days. It looked like one night's use was all it was going to get.

Maybe these two were former military, and never left things in a mess. Or maybe they hadn't brought a lot because they weren't sure what they would find.

But the lack of personal items—here and in the cavern—bothered him.

He carried minimal amounts of things when he was doing what he called a "quick and dirty," a job that would require him to go in and come out within 24 Earth hours.

This looked like a quick and dirty to him, right down to the items left in the building.

If the experts had to leave quickly, they could abandon the things they had here with no consequences at all. A few items of clothing, some cheap jewelry, nothing that couldn't be easily replaced.

Nothing that would be missed.

He shivered now, even though he had gotten warm.

What were they planning?

Why were they here?

And, most important of all, what did Dr. Reese know, and why hadn't she told him?

23

Navi let Roye go into the passageway first. She dreaded it, which surprised her. He had mentioned getting caught or trapped inside the passages before they dove, and now the idea was stuck in her head.

Everything seemed stuck in her head. Her teeth ached, and the ache was traveling up her cheekbones into her forehead. She would have a blinding headache before this was through if she didn't stop grinding her teeth together.

Roye's lights reflected off the white walls, coming back toward her like a halo. She dove into that instead of the darkness, swimming for the first time since they'd gone underwater.

At least the white sediment had thinned. Now it looked like they were going through actual water, not some kind of snowstorm.

Roye moved slowly ahead of her, his feet kicking just enough to propel him forward. She followed far enough behind that his moving feet wouldn't hit her.

She hadn't asked him if this place made him uneasy. She didn't want to admit it to herself.

So far they had found nothing.

She was beginning to wonder if they would find anything at all.

24

GABRIELLE WIPED THE LAST OF THE DIRT OFF A TINY vase. The vase was fragile, the glass so thin that a press of her fingers would crack it. Amazing it had survived this long underground. Amazing that digging it up hadn't harmed it in anyway.

Amazing that she even held it at all.

She was in the cleaning station at the back of the temple. So far, she was the only one to use this building. Even then, she hadn't brought the most precious items in here, like the statue she had found in the caverns. She didn't want to get into the habit.

She knew she would have to allow the others in soon, but she didn't want to.

She didn't want the interns and the post-docs and the eager young graduate students to see all of her treasures.

Of course, they wouldn't see *all* of her treasures. Some she would move to her own building, without ever having crossed the threshold here.

But even the small vases, insignificant except that they had come from the City of Denon and were a great example of Denonite workmanship, felt like hers.

She could sell this little thing for a small fortune, enough to retire on, and no one would ever know. She could sell the two dozen tiny vases already recovered, replenishing her finances as the years went by, and she would never get caught.

Collectors never told. They just enjoyed.

The problem was that she didn't want to retire. She loved the work in the field as much as she loved the treasures.

And she loved having her name attached to a major discovery—a discovery that would forever change not just the field of archeology, but the fields of history and art history. A discovery that might even help the humans in this sector recover the knowledge they had lost.

She held the vase up to the light flowing in from the door. The glass was so fine, she could see through it. It was so milky white, so dainty, that she had a hunch it was made from the white dirt that covered the top of the mountain.

As she stared through the vase, a shadow appeared.

Someone had come inside.

She sighed, and set the vase down.

Of course, the person violating her privacy was the stupid head of security, Meklos Verr.

Eventually, he would leave her alone.

Eventually, he would leave.

"Your experts have made a fascinating discovery," he said.

Her heart leaped. She had been hoping for this, but she hadn't wanted it to come through him. She wanted it to come from Yusef down in the cavern.

She carefully set the vase down—she didn't want to break it in her excitement—and stepped off the newly constructed floor. The tips of her shoes touched the edge of the drawing on the temple floor.

But Meklos didn't stand on the drawing, even though on previous occasions, he had walked all over it. He stayed at the other end of it, forcing her to walk to him.

She almost didn't. She almost made him come to her.

But she was too excited over the idea of a discovery. She wanted to see it, whatever it was.

"Aren't they early?" she asked. "Was there trouble? Why are they back so soon?"

"They aren't back," he said. "I found out about this by going through their packs."

The disappointment hit her like a physical blow.

She made sure her tone was cool. "I thought you had already searched the packs."

"I did," he said. "But I hadn't turned on their extra diving suit."

"They have an extra suit?" she asked.

He shrugged. "In case one got damaged, I would suppose. They form to whatever body puts them on."

She nodded. She'd seen suits like that in some of the space vessels she'd traveled on. She had even worn one, since one of the captains on one of her early trips wanted to make certain everyone knew how to put one on.

"So?"

"So," he said, "this one comes fitted with a map."

"A map?" she asked.

"Of the caverns."

"I never gave them a map of the caverns," she said. "We don't have one."

He studied her for a moment, as if he didn't believe her. "Are you sure about that?"

"Why the hell do you think I've sent them below?" she snapped. "It's not because I enjoy spending money. I need to know what's down there, and right now, I don't."

He nodded. The nod was tiny, and she wasn't even sure she was meant to see it. It seemed like a private nod, meant for him alone.

"Well," he said after a moment. "You know part of what's down there."

"Of course I do," she said. "Just like you do. We've been in the dry caverns—"

"No," he said. "You're standing on it."

She frowned, then looked down. She was standing on the reproduction of the Spires of Denon.

"What are you saying?"

He crouched and put his finger alongside one of the curves. "When I turned on the suit, this appeared. Only it was in outline only and three dimensional, like the Spires are above. And it had one added feature."

She walked toward him so that she could see what he was doing.

"Right here," he said, "was a small red dot. Right here."

One of the widest points of the Spires.

"When I moved the suit," he said, "the dot moved."

Like a directional device.

"It fits." With his finger, he traced the bottom part of the Spires. The drawing was wider here than at any other point. The circles crowded in on each other and eventually were separated by branches.

Passageways.

"If you overlay the map you have of the existing caves, you'll see that they're identical to this drawing," he said.

"That's not possible," she said. But she didn't mean that it was impossible to have this be a map. She was surprised, yes, but not that surprised.

He was right; the bottom part of this drawing did outline the caverns.

"It's possible," he said, somewhat defensively.

"No, no," she said. "That's not what I meant."

Then she realized she couldn't explain what she meant. She meant it was impossible for a lowly security guard, no matter how inflated his opinion was of himself, could make a discovery that she had missed.

"What did you mean then?" he asked.

She shook her head. "I meant," she lied, "I wonder how they knew."

25

THE NEXT CAVERN WAS OBVIOUSLY SMALLER. NAVI COULD see that from the passageway. Roye's light hit the walls, the ceiling, and the floor all at the same time, showing the entire cavern.

She could even see the passageway beyond.

The floor held nothing, so far as she could tell. There were niches, just like there'd been in the other caverns, but if she were a betting woman, she would bet they were empty.

Still, she would have to check them out.

Roye had moved toward one wall. She kicked slightly to propel herself forward, and veered a little to the left.

She grabbed the edge of the passageway's opening with one covered hand, planning to use the wall to push herself into the cavern.

Instead a thrumming echoed through her head. Her hand shook off the wall, and the violence of it sent her tumbling backwards.

Her entire body felt like it was being vibrated apart.

On one of her spins, she saw Roye, bent in half, his hands over his ears, even though the suit covered them.

What the hell? she said, but doubted Roye could hear her.

He shook his head—maybe he had heard her—and then looked toward her.

Sediment was filling the water.

Sediment—and something else—something coming out of the top of the passageway door.

26

SIRENS WENT OFF AND—JUST AS MEKLOS WAS GOING TO ask what was causing the sound (and why had Dr. Reese set up such a system, since they were worried about the vibrations destroying the Spires)—light flared.

Reflexively, he covered his eyes, and then he forced himself to open them.

A small line on the Spires drawing near his feet was glowing, the light so bright that he had to blink to keep the tears out of his eyes.

He looked up and saw that the ceiling of the temple had become porous, and through it, he thought he saw a similar light on the Spires themselves.

"Make it stop!" Dr. Reese shouted. "You'll ruin the Spires."

Her shout sounded like a whisper. He didn't want to answer her—it would take more effort than she deserved.

Instead, he ran outside. The light seemed worse than it had a moment ago, as if the sun had become even brighter. He shielded his eyes and made himself look up.

Sure enough, one small part of the Spires was glowing, sending light down to the temple, to the map that the Denonites had built in the temple floor.

He couldn't see the Spires clearly enough from below, not clearly enough to understand what he was looking at, so he went back inside the temple.

The single line glowed and so did one of the circles beyond. It wasn't very far from the first caverns that the divers would have gone into underwater.

A series of caverns, and then a passageway, and then another cavern. The passageway and the cavern had lit up.

"My God," Meklos said. "It's not artwork at all."

"What?" Dr. Reese had somehow managed to join him. Her eyes were small pinpoints of blackness in her pale face. "What's not art?"

"The Spires," he said. "They're not art or a map or anything like that. They're a defense system."

27

A BARRIER DESCENDED FROM THE TOP OF THE PASSAGEWAY door. The barrier was milk-colored and opaque, like the water, and it came down with great force.

Navi thought it should have shattered as it hit the ground. Then she realized that had her hand been in the way, the sharp bottom of that barrier would have sliced it off.

She whirled, not wanting to be trapped in the passageway. But nothing had come down behind her. She looked up, and the ceiling of the passage looked fine.

She was disturbing the water, making the sediment rise around her, but otherwise she was fine.

The vibrating had stopped. All the shaking and thrumming and violence had ended when the barrier connected with the bottom of the passage.

Roye? She sent to him. *Roye?*

She could see him through the barrier. He looked a little smaller than he was. He had swum to the barrier between them.

He tapped his head—he couldn't hear her or communicate with her. He had to be trying, just like she was.

They both grabbed the sides of the passageway, just like she had before, feeling for something, anything, that would make the barrier rise again.

Only she hadn't pressed her hands flat against anything. She had grabbed the curve in the doorway, the wall itself, separating the passage from the cavern.

She had activated something.

And now she had to shut it off.

She held up a finger, then swam back to the caverns they had explored before.

The first cavern looked no different, except that there might have been more sediment floating in the water.

She had to force herself to breathe slowly, to calm herself, so that she didn't swim through the caverns and out.

She swam back into the passageway, even though it made her cringe.

Roye was still trying to figure out how to open the damn thing. He didn't look panicked, not like she felt.

But how could she tell? She could only see his eyes, through the clear part of his suit and even that was through this weird milky barrier.

She resumed touching the sides as well. If only she could remember exactly where she had put her hand, she might be able to touch the edge of whatever it was.

Her heart was racing and she was breathing too rapidly. Her suit would shut her down soon if she wasn't careful. It would start regulating her air.

She concentrated on touching the wall. One hand overlapping the other, moving slowly.

Moving deliberately.

Trying to find a way to get Roye out.

28

THE SIRENS STOPPED. MEKLOS'S EARS RANG.

He looked down. The light remained, the line glowing, the cavern glowing, and a smaller blackish silvery light threading out of the little area between them.

"Did we have a groundquake?" Dr. Reese asked.

He frowned. He hadn't noticed, with the light and the sound and the Spires glowing above them.

"Was that real vibration or was it caused by the sound?" she asked.

Her words still sounded tinny and far away. Those sirens had been loud. He looked up. The ceiling was still porous. The light was still flowing down, and he could almost see that silvery blackness in the center of it.

She shook her head at him in exasperation, then staggered away from him, toward the back. He had a hunch she was talking, but he had no idea what she was saying.

He didn't care.

If this was some kind of defense system, then the divers had set it off.

And if they had set it off, then they were in trouble.

He left the temple at full run.

29

THE LITTLE VASE HAD SHATTERED. IT HAD VIBRATED OFF her worktable and landed on the newly installed floor. Gabrielle knelt, removing tiny slivers of glass, her heart aching.

If she had left the vase in the niche near the door of the house she had chosen to live in, the vase would be fine now. It wouldn't have fallen.

It wouldn't have broken.

All those centuries, only to have her carelessness destroy it.

But, as she held the larger shards in the palm of her hand, she realized she could test it now. She could see if the glass had truly been made from the white dirt near the Spires.

The Spires. What had Meklos said? That they were a defense system? Which meant that they made that noise.

Impossible.

She cupped the shards in her hand, grabbed a small box that still remained on her worktable, and poured the shards into the box. Then she used a cloth to gently wipe off her palm.

Her ears rang.

Maybe the fall hadn't broken the vase. Maybe the sound had shattered it.

Just like it would have shattered the Spires.

Her breath caught.

She set the cloth down. Shattered the Spires and sent them tumbling to the ground, causing the quake.

She was probably lucky nothing had hit the temple. Even though she really didn't recognize this place, with the debris on the floor, the light emanating from one small part of the painting, and the open ceiling, which was letting the light through.

She had panicked and now she wasn't. Now she was thinking clearly.

She made herself walk out of the temple, avoiding the artwork on the floor just because it made her nervous.

The whole thing made her nervous.

She had never experienced anything like this, not in all her years as an archeologist and leader of expeditions.

The sunlight blinded her. She blinked away tears, then wiped her eyes. Finally she looked at the area around her.

Even after the quake, it looked the same. Nothing had fallen here. Nothing had broken.

She expected to see bits of the Spires all over the city, crushing buildings, ruining all her hard work.

But she saw nothing different.

Except a small amount of dust floating in the air, as if it had been dislodged from the dust piles.

She steeled herself, straightening her shoulders, stiffening her back.

Then she looked up.

The Spires were so bright that they hurt her eyes. Light flowed from them to the temple itself.

But the Spires hadn't crumbled. They hadn't fallen apart. All that worry about sound and vibration and powerful equipment had been completely wrong.

The Spires were sturdy.

They were sending light to the temple, through the open ceiling, and onto that little two-dimensional drawing on the floor. White light threaded with black.

Like the drawing.

Meklos had said it was a map.

And if it was a map, then something had just triggered it. Something had turned it on.

The light had appeared in the area where the divers were.

She cursed.

How was she supposed to deal with the fact that the security guard—a lowly security guard—had seen something she and her team had missed for years?

She shook her head. She couldn't think about that now. She needed to figure out what to do next.

30

ROYE HAD BROUGHT A SCANNER. HE HELD IT UP AGAINST the barrier. The scanner was small, barely the size of his fingers, and if Navi hadn't known what it was, she wouldn't have recognized it.

He ran it along the edge of the barrier.

She hadn't brought any equipment, not like that. She had believed Dr. Reese's experts—that this place was incredibly fragile, and needed protection from all sorts of equipment.

If this place was fragile, then it should have fallen apart from the vibration as the barrier came down.

It hadn't.

Still, she was here with only her suit's sensors.

They would have to do.

She opened the palm of her right hand and surveyed the wall holding the barrier in place. Equipment yes, but no controls. The controls, so far as her small scanner could tell, had to be somewhere else.

She methodically moved her hand along the edge, searching for some kind of device, any kind, to release the barrier.

After all, she had triggered it from here. She had to be able to release it from here as well.

Roye ran his scan along his side. He finished before she did, then started all over again.

When she was finally done, she looked at him through the barrier. His face was distorted by the water and the glass-like material. His eyes looked too big in their clear protective area.

He shook his head.

So did she.

What had she triggered?

She put her palm on the side again and this time, got a small hit.

This part of the wall was touch-sensitive. She had triggered something, but nothing in the wall itself. The touch system had sent a signal elsewhere and that signal told the system to lower the barrier.

Then she frowned. Slowly she raised her hand to her mouth.

Her teeth didn't ache any more. Neither did her head.

She had been feeling some kind of energy field. Either the barrier had cut the field off, or the field had shut off when she touched the wall.

She couldn't remember when her teeth stopped aching. It was hard to notice an absence of pain.

She tapped the barrier. Roye looked at her, startled.

She put a finger to her cheek and hoped he could understand what she meant since they could no longer communicate. She couldn't mouth anything at him, and she couldn't point to her own teeth.

She tapped her cheek again, then held out her hands in a question.

He stared at her for a moment, then he seemed to understand. He ran a hand along his chin, then stopped. He shook his head. Then he shrugged.

She wasn't sure what that meant. Was the pain still there? Or was it gone?

She shrugged.

He made a circle with his fist. Zero. He didn't feel anything.

Neither did she.

She nodded.

So the barrier hadn't broken the field, leaving it working on his side and off on hers. The field had just gone away.

Maybe she hadn't triggered it when she touched the wall. Maybe Roye had when he swam through the opening.

Or maybe the only part of the field that still worked was the wall area. The water might have damaged the rest.

She pointed at her finger, as if she held the small scanner he had brought. It took him a moment, but he finally held it up.

She nodded.

Then she pointed behind him.

It took a few more gestures before he realized what she wanted.

She wanted him to scan the passages behind him, see if there were more barriers. He held up a finger and swam away from her.

The water swirled where he had been. There was definitely more sediment in it now, and that intrigued her. It meant something, although she wasn't sure what.

She waited, holding her breath until she realized what she was doing. When she finally released it, she saw him swimming back toward her.

He was nodding. It looked like his eyes were crinkling in the corners. Did that mean he was grinning?

He mimed swimming, then pointed behind him. Then he pointed behind her. She nodded.

They were each going to swim away from the barrier. Obviously as far as he could scan, there were no obvious barriers.

She doubted there were any on her side either.

But if there were, she would wait near one of them for him to come get her. Because once they got out of this godforsaken underground lair, they'd communicate with each other, Spires be damned.

And then they'd get the hell out of here.

He waved at her. She waved back.

Then he whirled and swam away from the barrier.

After a moment, she did the same thing, swimming back the way they came.

31

MEKLOS WENT DOWN THE ANCIENT STEPS FIVE AT A time, until he slipped and had to catch himself with a hand on the ice-cold wall. The steps were covered with white dust, which was as slick as water.

He made his way down the remaining steps carefully until he reached the cavern where Yusef was waiting for the divers to return.

For a moment, Meklos didn't see Yusef. He didn't see the packs either, and thought he was in the wrong place.

Then he realized they were all covered in dust.

He hurried across the floor. Yusef leaned against the wall, his heavy coat white, his face so dust-covered it looked like it was coated in ice.

"You all right?" Meklos asked.

Yusef opened his eyes. He focused on Meklos and then his eyes filled with tears.

"My ears," Yusef said too loudly. He reached toward them with his uncovered hand. The fingertips were black. Why wasn't he wearing gloves?

Meklos turned Yusef's head. Blood had oozed out of his ears and frozen onto the side of his head. His fingertips were probably not frostbitten; they were probably covered in blood.

"Can't stand," Yusef said, again speaking much too loud. "I'm so dizzy."

The siren must have been particularly loud in here. Whether the cavern was the source or whether the sound had just echoed off the enclosed space—and the water—Meklos didn't know.

"I'll get you out," Meklos said.

He didn't want to. He wanted to make sure the divers were all right. But he had to take care of this man first.

"Can you stand?" Meklos asked.

Yusef put a finger up toward his ear again. "I can't hear you."

His eardrums must have ruptured. Meklos didn't even want to think about that kind of pain.

"Can you stand?" Meklos asked slowly, making sure his mouth formed each word carefully.

"I think so," Yusef said. He struggled to his feet, using the wall to brace himself.

Meklos slipped his arm around Yusef's back and half-carried him toward the stairs.

The slippery stairs.

This would take longer than he wanted it to. But he had to do it.

Then he would come back for the divers.

If it wasn't too late.

32

Navi swam into the larger cavern, happy to be out of the passageways. She didn't try to walk this time. She wasn't moving slowly. She was swimming as hard as she could.

The cavern looked bigger than it had on the way in, but that was probably because Roye wasn't with her. His presence had put the place into perspective, giving her something to concentrate on besides the snowy water and the curving walls.

She had nothing to concentrate on now except getting the hell out of here.

She slowed as she reached the first archway, and gingerly extended her hand toward it.

They had both touched the walls in here, looking for niches or anything that could be valuable, and they hadn't set anything off.

So either that other cavern had been more valuable or the barriers didn't exist this far in.

She made herself concentrate on her fingers, reaching, reaching—

—and finding nothing. They slipped into the next cavern, just like they had on the way in.

She swam through, her heart pounding.

Why have barriers on that side? Why not here?

She couldn't figure it out.

But it kept her brain busy while she swam to the next cavern.

It kept her busy while she did her best to get out.

33

"WE HAVE TO FIGURE OUT HOW TO SHUT THIS OFF," Gabrielle said. She was standing on the temple steps. Most of her team had gathered here, apparently looking for instruction.

If they wanted instruction, she'd give it to them.

She waved her hand at the wave of light. "This thing could be dangerous."

The light bath that she enjoyed every day hadn't been a brighter moment in the sun. The system had run some kind of program, one she was too stupid to understand.

She'd never been inside the temple when it ran. She had always come outside to bathe in the light.

If she had been inside, would she have seen that the temple's ceiling grew clear, and the light illuminated parts of the drawing below?

She had no idea, and she couldn't think about it now.

"There's a silvery black thread running through the light," she said. "I don't like it. I've never seen it before."

She didn't tell them that the light illuminated the drawing inside or that the drawing was really a map. Nor did she tell them Meklos's theory that the entire thing— the Spires, the map, the temple—was some kind of defense system.

"I'm convinced though," she said, "that this is all man-made. If there's a way to turn it on—and something clearly did—then there's a way to turn it off. We have to find it."

"The light is focused on the temple," said one of the graduate students. "Does that mean the controls are inside?'

How am I supposed to know, you ass? she nearly snapped, but she caught herself just in time.

"Maybe," she said. "Or maybe there's something near the Spires. Spread out and look. Those of you with engineering experience, look around here first. Use scanners and communicators. If the Spires can survive that loud siren, they can survive anything."

She hoped.

It was all a guess now.

And so far, at least when it came to the Spires of Denon, all of her previous guesses had been wrong.

34

By the time they reached the ground floor of the building that hid the cavern's entrance, Meklos was carrying Yusef. The man had fainted halfway up, which was probably a blessing.

Meklos carried him through the door and into the street. Several members of Dr. Reese's team were running by.

"Hey! Hey!" he shouted. "I need help here."

Chavo stopped. So did two others.

"He needs a doctor," Meklos said. "Get him to the doctor. And send my people here. They need to go to the caves."

"Caves?" Chavo asked.

So Dr. Reese hadn't told the rest of her team.

"Caves," Meklos said. "Through this door is an entrance leading down. I need at least three of my people, preferably the ones who can dive."

"Dive?" Chavo asked.

"Just tell Phin that," Meklos said, realizing he had no time to explain. "He'll understand."

Meklos passed Yusef off to two of the students, then ran back into the building. He heard steps behind him, turned, and saw Chavo.

"I gave you instructions," Meklos snapped.

"I just didn't believe it. Do you think the controls are in here?"

"What controls?" Meklos asked.

"For the light," Chavo said.

"I don't care," Meklos said. "Go get Phin. I need help here—experienced help—and I need it now. You got that? You can search for whatever it is you're searching for after you get me some assistance."

"Yes, sir," Chavo said and sprinted for the door.

Meklos was halfway down the stairs before he realized what Chavo was talking about.

The controls for the defense system. Dr. Reese must have sent them in search of the controls.

Stupid woman. Didn't she realize that a group of dirt scientists wouldn't know anything about ancient technology?

If they found controls, they might make things worse.

But he kept going down into the cold.

He needed to get those divers out before the archeologists screwed things up again.

35

Finally, Navi's head rose above the water. She let out a relieved breath and almost removed her suit, then remembered how cold this cavern was.

It was completely empty. She thought Gabrielle Reese had left someone to watch for them, but no one was in the cavern. And their packs were gone.

She swam until she had to walk, and then she hurried out of the water, her breath coming in small gasps. As she got closer to the water's edge, she scanned the cavern.

It looked like the one she had left, but she wasn't sure. Caverns could look alike down here, with their niches and their archways—

And the stairs.

Not only were there stairs, but the stairs had footprints, going up, coming down and going up.

She made her gaze follow the footprints until she saw a huge disturbance in the cavern floor. It was right next to the wall, near where the water ended.

Someone had been sitting there, and someone else had come down. One set of footprints came down, and two went up, although one seemed like that person dragged their feet.

The fact she could see prints registered for the first time. The water wasn't the only thing filled with more sediment. The walls had flaked, and the flaking had been severe.

The flakes had fallen throughout the cavern like snow.

Which meant that this had happened before. Because of the sediment in the water. That had come from somewhere before the barrier came down.

She stepped out of the water, and searched for her pack. It had to be here. It was probably just covered in sediment.

The sediment clung to her feet and legs, coating her in white. As she disturbed it, more and more covered her.

Then she heard something from above.

She looked up. A man came down the stairs, sideways, holding the wall.

The man's head suddenly came into view. It was Meklos Verr, the head of security.

The competent one.

She let out the breath she was holding, relieved.

"Oh, thank god," she said, and realized her voice was muffled by the suit. She pulled it off her face.

The air wasn't just cold.

It was frigid.

"Where's your partner?" Meklos said. "Is he all right?"

"I think so," she said. "We'll know soon enough."

"What does that mean?" He finally reached the bottom part of the cavern. "Is he behind you?"

"No," she said, then glanced at the water.

"Then where is he?"

If she told Meklos, she would have to tell him about the map. She would have to explain her scans. She would probably have to admit who she was.

She glanced at the stairs.

"Are you alone?" she asked.

"At the moment. I sent for reinforcements. Some members of my team have water diving experience. I was going to use your extra suit."

Something passed across his face then. His expression sharpened for just a moment.

"The suit," he said, "adjusts to the wearer, doesn't it?"

She nodded.

"And you can stay underwater for a very long time," he said.

"It's designed for that," she said.

"So you and one of my team can get him."

She shook her head. "We probably won't have to."

She hoped they wouldn't have to. She never wanted to go into that water again.

"You triggered something down there," he said.

"A barrier. Roye was on one side, and I was on the other."

"So he went out the passageway to the ship you have waiting."

She blinked at him, not sure if she had heard him correctly.

"I found your map," he said. "How did you get that?"

She had heard him. This day was full of surprises.

"He'll contact me when he gets out," she said, choosing not to answer Meklos's question. "I'm not sure how long to wait."

"What were you planning to do? Rob the lower caverns? Take all the loot and fly it out of here without any of us being wiser?" He took a step toward her. "What even made you think there's something down in those caverns?"

"There's nothing in those caverns," she said.

"You know that now," he said. "But you thought something was down there before."

"I did," she said. "I was told this might be a museum. For the Denonites. They would have used it for all the spoils of the various wars they fought."

"And you came to rob it," Meklos said.

"I came to save it," she said.

He glared at her. "Really?"

"Really," she said.

"How did you plan to do that?" he asked.

She took a deep breath. She was going to have to trust him. "By getting enough evidence to arrest Dr. Gabrielle Reese."

36

A LIGHT WAS MOVING ALONG THE INTERIOR LINES OF the Spires. Gabrielle had gone inside the temple to watch. Looking up at the Spires hurt her eyes, but in here, in the dimness, she could see the light move.

It moved as if someone were shining a light source on a particular area. Then, once that area received a thorough examination, the source moved to the next area.

If she hadn't learned long ago that there were no light sources underneath the drawing of the Spires (at least none that she recognized), she would have thought someone was playing with lights underneath the floor.

The movement unnerved her. The way everything had changed in just the past hour had unnerved her.

Her staff crowded parts of the temple. They were using scanners and talking loudly. Before people had spoken in hushed tones here. Now the voices were raised, excited, the way people talked when they were panicked and thrilled at the same time.

Her team thought this new development interesting.

It worried her.

Not just because it could be dangerous. Hell, it *was* dangerous. She had seen Yusef as the staff carried him to their doctor. He was so pale she thought he had died. Blood blackened both of his ears, and his lips were blue.

Something had happened in that cavern. Chavo ventured a guess that the sound was magnified down there. But she wasn't so sure.

She wasn't sure about anything.

She wasn't even sure why that light was moving.

The only thing she could tell was that it was heading away from the caverns.

And she couldn't figure out why that would happen either.

She rubbed her hands over her upper arms, feeling the gooseflesh along her skin.

In all her years digging and searching, finding ancient burial sites, ancient *treasure,* she had never experienced anything like this.

And she never wanted to experience anything like it again.

37

"ARREST DOCTOR REESE?" MEKLOS COULDN'T KEEP the shock from his voice. He'd researched Dr. Reese before taking this job. Even though she wasn't yet forty, she had discovered several important sites, including this one. She'd made large contributions to the fields of archeology, art history, and general history in this sector.

Granted, she was a loner and not always liked by her crews, but that hadn't bothered him. Most people in positions of power weren't liked.

Although he hadn't liked her either, partly because of her attitude and partly because she had hid information from him.

Like these caves.

"Yes, we were looking for reasons to arrest her." Salvino had found the packs. She picked one up, making the sediment float around her like a dust storm. Some of the whiteness adhered to her right thigh, her belly, and her lower arm.

Then she let the pack fall. She opened her suit, and slowly pulled it off, sliding it off her right arm and hand first, and then going to her left.

Meklos was torn between two questions. He wanted more information on Dr. Reese and this startling announcement.

But, over the years, he had learned that startling announcements were often diversionary tactics, to make a questioner forget his line of questioning.

He had asked Salvino if she was going to rob the artifacts from this area, just before she had said she was going to prevent a robbery. She hadn't answered his first question.

So he decided against pursuing that tack and went for the other.

"I checked you out," he said, not adding that he had done it as best he could in a limited amount of time. "You're a cave diver, not a police officer."

"Technically, I'm neither." Salvino stepped out of the suit. It crumpled against the ground. The water dripping off it made a little trail back to the pool.

Then she opened her pack. She slid her hand inside, grasped a seam, and peeled it back.

Meklos cursed. How had he missed that? Not once, but twice.

She glanced at him. "You couldn't have found it without very specialized equipment," she said as if she were reading his thoughts. "It's keyed to my DNA, and my DNA only. That's why I wasn't worried about leaving the pack behind. You'd never find this pouch and if you miraculously did, you'd never open it."

He pressed his lips together. He didn't believe in never. He would have gotten it open, eventually.

She slipped her hand into the pouch and pulled something out. It was some kind data on drive as thin as a fingernail.

She handed it to him, but he didn't have a scanner on him.

"What this will tell you," she said, "is that I'm Navi Salvino of the Interagency Arts and Monuments Protection League. We're a squad of investigators authorized by various governments, including the Unified Governments of Amnthra, to protect historic sites and properties throughout the sector. If we do find a problem, we turn that problem over to the enforcement arm best equipped to handle that problem."

He slipped the small dataport into a pocket of his shirt, and sealed that pocket. He'd heard of the Interagency Arts and Monuments Protection League mostly by its acronym IAMPL. In the last decade, they'd stopped some spectacular thefts throughout the sector.

But that didn't mean she was a legitimate part of the organization. Only that she had heard of it, along with everyone else in the sector.

"Dr. Reese has a fantastic reputation," Meklos said.

"I'm sure you noted that when you decided to take this job," Salvino said. "You probably also noted that she had a significant amount of money in various accounts."

He had. He hadn't thought much of it. She was an in-demand expert in her field, a woman who commanded high prices for almost anything she did.

"That wasn't my concern."

"It was ours." Salvino pulled the thin heating blanket from her pack. She flapped the blanket open, then wrapped it around herself. "No matter how well known they are, people in Dr. Reese's position don't make a great deal of money. Everything they do is paid for. The Scholars funded this expedition, and will continue to fund it for all the years of its lifetime. They funded her previous expeditions as well."

"So?" Meklos was getting cold. He'd run around a great deal since the sirens went off, sweating through his clothes. Now the clammy material was starting to freeze. "That proves nothing."

"In and of itself, you're right." Salvino pushed her hair out of her face. Her hand was trembling. "But we also found a lot of small items with dubious provenance that we could later trace back to her earlier digs. At some point, she takes items from her sites and sends them through a series of dealers. She sells these small items to private buyers for a great deal of money."

"I don't know how she could," Meklos said. "This dig is well known."

But as he spoke, he understood. The dig was well known, but the location of the so-called museum wasn't. If the caverns were as billed, then Dr. Reese could have taken items from here before they were ever recorded. They would have been deemed lost, if they were even known.

She hadn't told him about the caverns. She didn't want her assistants down here. From Chavo's reaction, he hadn't known about the cavern either.

She had been keeping secrets.

Too many of them.

"You're beginning to understand," Salvino said.

"Or you're lying to me to cover up your own plan."

She sighed. "My plan was simple. I wanted to get into this dig to see if there were valuables to loot. The cave diving was a gift. Then we were able to map the caverns, and—"

"How did you map the caverns?" he asked. "Dr. Reese didn't."

"Dr. Reese was afraid of her site," Salvino said. "She didn't want to use equipment because of the Spires."

"You believe that?" he asked. It could have been a good excuse to keep everyone else from finding the caverns below.

"Yes, I believe that," Salvino said. She picked up her suit, folded it, and shoved it into her pack. "All the scientists worried that the Spires were too fragile to handle much of anything."

He had seen that in some of his research.

"We decided to try scanning from the ground, just outside the secure zone. But we were looking for the caverns." Salvino picked up the other pack. The blanket started to slide off her shoulders. "No one else ever did."

Meklos put the blanket around her, then took both packs. "How did you know about the caverns?" he asked.

"We didn't. But when I realized we were going to see the Spires, I hired an expert, a man by the name of Zeigler—"

"I've heard of him," Meklos said.

She gave Meklos a measuring look. "Then you know why I trusted his instinct. It turned out to be right."

Meklos nodded. He would check Salvino out, but her explanations made a lot of sense.

"Lying about your cave diving experience could have killed you," he said.

She shook her head. "Nothing in my information packet was a lie. I've dived a lot, mostly on jobs like this. You'd be surprised how many ancient cities are flooded."

"Nothing was a lie," he repeated. "But you left out a lot."

"I erased everything that was important, figuring no one would bother to check. I was right."

His cheeks warmed. "I checked," he said. "But the equipment here—"

"Worked to my advantage," she said. Her teeth were chattering.

"What's your plan now?" he asked. "Go to the surface and arrest Dr. Reese?"

"No," Salvino said. "There's no reason. The caverns are empty."

"So you say," Meklos said. "There's no way to check. For all I know, your companion is taking valuables out now."

"I'll let you check our ship," she said. "You can examine everything we have."

He gave her a measuring look. She seemed truthful, but he had no real way to know.

Although deep down, he trusted her.

And he had never trusted Dr. Reese.

38

As they climbed the stairs, Meklos explained what happened above ground to Navi. He explained his defense system theory.

It made sense.

It made her disappointment fade.

She had wanted to see the museum. But that didn't exist—or no longer existed, at least not here. The defense system was almost as good, maybe better, since it probably had applications in the modern era.

And it would prevent Gabrielle Reese from robbing this place blind—if, indeed, there was anything to steal.

Because she wouldn't be in charge any longer.

The Scholars got most of their funding from government grants from all over the sector. Various governments would want to know how this defense system worked. They'd bid for the rights to study it.

This entire place would become famous. Dr. Reese wouldn't have untrammeled access any longer.

They had nearly reached the top of the stairs when Navi put her hand on Meklos's arm.

"Check me out," she said. "As soon as we get to the surface. If what you say is true, then you can use proper communications equipment right from the city and it won't cause any harm. With a more powerful system, you'll see my bio, even without the disk I gave you. You'll find it all."

He stopped beside her, moving the packs to one hand. "Why should I do that?"

"Because we're going to hire you. You'll guard this place for us until we can bring in reinforcements and take control from Dr. Reese."

"She found this place. By your own admission, she hasn't done anything," he said. "You were right. There is no reason to take her off the dig."

Navi smiled. "I'm glad you understand. She truly is a gifted expert in her field. She should be allowed to stay. But you need to make sure everything else stays as well."

He grunted, which she took as an assent. Although she wasn't sure.

She climbed the remaining steps into the building. People combed the walls, scanning everything.

The site looked completely different than it had in the morning.

"Are there really caves down there?" one of the graduate students asked her.

The kid was so excited he apparently didn't noticed the white all over her clothing or the blanket around her shoulders. Or the way her teeth were chattering.

"I'm not at liberty to say," Navi said. She let Meklos lead her into the sunshine.

The warm sunshine that seemed to have a life of its own. It undulated like water toward the building that Gabrielle Reese had called the temple.

Clearly that wasn't a temple at all, but some kind of central control station.

"You want to see it?" Meklos asked her.

Navi nodded. She wanted to see it, then she wanted to go back to the building she'd been staying in. She wanted to sit alone in the darkness and shake.

She wanted a few minutes to let the fear ease away before she had to be completely professional again.

39

THE LIGHT WAS ALMOST TO THE END OF THE SPIRES NOW. Gabrielle studied the light moving through the two-dimensional drawing as if it were alive and about to attack.

A few of her team had gathered around as well, asking questions that she mostly ignored.

Then Meklos came inside. People parted from him as if he were going to harm them. He had a woman with him, and it took Gabrielle a moment to realize it was one of the divers.

"What did you find?" she asked, barely able to control her excitement. The museum? Treasures? She wasn't sure she could hide any of it now, but that mattered less than the fact of the artifacts. She wanted to see the famous Spoils of War Museum that the Denonites had created.

"Nothing," the woman said. She sounded tired.

"It's a long story," Meklos said. Obviously, he already knew what the story was.

Gabrielle glared at him. He was still getting in her way.

But he didn't seem to notice her glare. Instead, he was staring at the drawing.

"This is brilliant," he said to the diver. "This is how the Denonites protected themselves against siege. Those passages below had to have once been easily visible from the ground. The Denonites built this so that they could track anyone entering."

"And prevent them from coming into the city with those barriers," the diver said.

"What barriers?" Gabrielle asked.

But they ignored her. She wasn't used to being ignored.

She was about to ask the question again, when the light moved to the last part of a Spire. It flickered for a moment, and then disappeared.

There was a grinding above her.

The ceiling closed.

The lights were gone.

"What was that?" she asked.

But she didn't expect anyone to answer her, so she hurried outside. The light no longer flowed down from the Spires.

The city looked normal—as normal as it had before the sirens went off.

The defense system had shut off, but she didn't know why. She was beginning to think she didn't know anything.

All her assumptions had been false.

She was torn between awe at the system she'd seen and a disconcerting sense of unease, as if life as she had known it had suddenly and irrevocably changed.

40

"He got out," Navi said softly. "He got out."

She felt more relief than she expected to.

"I'll give him a few minutes, and then contact the ship."

She looked at Meklos.

"I can't believe he got out."

Meklos smiled. He seemed calmer too. "He got out and the system shut off. This thing is brilliant. The threat is gone, so the entire system is back in wait mode."

"We're going to be studying this for a long time," Navi said. "Will you help?"

"When everything checks out," Meklos said.

She nodded. She understood that. She took her pack from Meklos, dug into the pouch, and grabbed her communicator.

Damn, it was nice to use a powerful system again.

She held it up to him. His smile widened.

She walked to the door. Gabrielle Reese was sitting on the stairs outside, looking like she was lost.

And she had lost. The woman was smart enough to know that the change in the Spires made the dig something completely different.

Oddly, Navi wanted to comfort her, to tell her that what she would lose financially, she would gain in reputation. Gabrielle Reese would forever be the woman who discovered the long-lost technology of the Denonites.

But Navi didn't say that. Instead she stepped into the street, bathing in the warmth of Amnthra's bright sun. She held up her communicator, pressing it on.

She didn't use any identifying words. The signal from the comm should have been enough.

"I'm checking on Roye," she said. "Is he all right?"

He looks like he's made of snow, the pilot of her deep exploration ship answered. *But he's all right. Glad to be out of there. You coming to join us?*

She looked over her shoulder. There were too many changes here, too much going on. Much as she trusted Meklos Verr, she had a hunch he didn't trust her.

And there was too much at stake to leave to a man she'd just hired.

"No, I'm staying here. I'll send up a full report tonight. We're going to need a lot of experts here very fast. And not the kind that we have. We're dealing with technology now, not ancient art."

Figured out that much, the pilot said. *Roye wants to know if you're all right. Does he need to come over the mountain to find you?*

"I'm fine," she said, then she took a deep breath of the warm air.

More than fine. She was thrilled.

Everything had turned out much better than she expected.

"Tell him," she said, "I'm just fine."

41

It didn't take Meklos long to check out Navi Salvino, now that he had the proper equipment. He spent most of his time digging through information logs from far away, ones she never would have thought to tamper with.

While he did that, Meklos had his team set up a better perimeter. He put robots and motion detectors all around the rim of the crater, like he'd wanted to do from the beginning.

He was going to ask if he could stay here. He wanted to study the Spires system. It fascinated him.

He'd been in countless cities that protected themselves from attack, but not like this place. He wanted to know more.

And he had a hunch there would always be more to know.

He lifted his face toward the Spires. He'd thought them beautiful when he first saw them.

But now he realized they were more than beautiful. They were fascinating and, more importantly, useful.

He smiled at them—and silently promised he would always keep them safe.

The adventure continues in Kristine Kathryn
Rusch's award-winning Diving Universe with
The Renegat, on sale now.

Be the first to know!

Just sign up for the Kristine Kathryn Rusch newsletter,
and keep up with the latest news, releases
and so much more—even the occasional giveaway.

So, what are you waiting for?
To sign up go to kristinekathrynrusch.com.

But wait! There's more. Sign up for the WMG
Publishing newsletter, too, and get the latest news
and releases from all of the WMG authors and lines,
including Kristine Grayson, Kris Nelscott, Dean
Wesley Smith, *Fiction River: An Original Anthology
Magazine, Pulphouse Fiction Magazine, Smith's
Monthly,* and so much more.

To sign up, go to wmgpublishing.com.

ABOUT THE AUTHOR

New York Times bestselling author Kristine Kathryn Rusch writes in almost every genre. Generally, she uses her real name (Rusch) for most of her writing. Under that name, she publishes bestselling science fiction and fantasy, award-winning mysteries, acclaimed mainstream fiction, controversial nonfiction, and the occasional romance. Her novels have made bestseller lists around the world and her short fiction has appeared in eighteen best of the year collections. She has won more than twenty-five awards for her fiction, including the Hugo, *Le Prix Imaginales*, the *Asimov's* Readers Choice award, and the *Ellery Queen Mystery Magazine* Readers Choice Award.

To keep up with everything she does, go to kriswrites.com and sign up for her newsletter. To track her many pen names and series, see their individual websites (krisnelscott.com, kristinegrayson.com, retrievalartist.com, divingintothewreck.com, fictionriver.com, pulphousemagazine.com).

The Retrieval Artist Universe
(Reading Order)

www.ingramcontent.com/pod-product-compliance
Lightning Source LLC
Chambersburg PA
CBHW020332110726
47898CB00003B/849